"Hungry for more than cookies?"

Brynn asked, looking far too pretty in faded cutoffs and a pink tank that accentuated full breasts. With her hair in braids, she looked fresh from Tristan's every naughty farm-girl fantasy.

He shook his head. "I'm sorry, but I really should get going."

What's wrong?" she asked, her voice raspy with what he could only guess was the same confusion dogging him. "You used to be the only person I could talk to—about anything. But ever since I had Mackenzie, you've been distant."

"Sorry. Truth is, with the baby, I feel awkward being around you."

"We can't be friends? Because that's all I'm asking for."

He cocked his head. "Really?"

Everything about her from her flirty stance to her full, pouty lips to her heightened color told him she was a woman amenable to being kissed. Lord help him, but Tristan was up for the job. But Brynn was hardly the one-night-stand kind of girl he dallied with back in Virginia Beach. They knew up front he was interested only in fun and they were okay with it. He suspected Brynn, on the other hand, didn't have a clue what she genuinely wanted—especially with regard to him....

Dear Reader,

As I'm writing this, we just celebrated Father's Day here in the States and of all the heroes I've written, Tristan faces some of the toughest parenting battles.

Since Hubby had to work, we opted for a low-key lunch out at our fave Mexican restaurant. Though we didn't do anything fancy, we still managed to at least share a meal and I got my requisite warm and fuzzies from being surrounded by most everyone I love.

Throughout this story, Tristan struggles with the fact that as a SEAL, his basic job requirement is that he isn't always going to be home. Early in our marriage, I used to get so frustrated when Hubby had overtime. Now, I realize how blessed we are that he has a job. How fortunate I am to have a wonderful man in my life who loves me and his children enough to sacrifice much of his free time to ensure our kids and I lead comfortable lives.

Happy Father's Day to all of the hardworking dads! Though I didn't get to make the trip to Arkansas to see my dad this year, he's always in my heart, and I know I'll see him soon.

Poor Tristan, however, doesn't know when—or if—he'll see the son he loves again. Will Brynn and her family be enough to help him through his pain? I'm not telling….

Happy reading!

Laura Marie

The SEAL's Valentine
LAURA MARIE ALTOM

HARLEQUIN®
entertain, enrich, inspire™

Recycling programs
for this product may
not exist in your area.

ISBN-13: 978-0-373-75439-7

THE SEAL'S VALENTINE

www.Harlequin.com

Printed in U.S.A.

ABOUT THE AUTHOR

After college (Go, Hogs!), bestselling, award-winning author Laura Marie Altom did a brief stint as an interior designer before becoming a stay-at-home mom to boy-girl twins and a bonus son. Always an avid romance reader, she knew it was time to try her hand at writing when she found herself replotting the afternoon soaps.

When not immersed in her next story, Laura teaches art at a local middle school. In her free time, she beats her kids at video games, tackles Mount Laundry and of course reads romance!

Laura loves hearing from readers at either P.O. Box 2074, Tulsa, OK 74101, or by email, BaliPalm@aol.com.

Love winning fun stuff? Check out www.lauramariealtom.com.

Books by Laura Marie Altom

HARLEQUIN AMERICAN ROMANCE

*U.S. Marshals
**Baby Boom
***The Buckhorn Ranch
‡Operation: Family

For my father, Edward Alisch, and the father of my sweet children, Terry Altom. I love you two! Thank you for all you do!

Chapter One

Come on, baby… You can do it.

Brynn Langtoine crossed her fingers so tightly her knuckles shone white. Six-year-old Cayden had already been through so much in losing his father, he just had to make a home run for his little league tryout. Or, she prayed, for once come close to at least hitting the ball.

The metal bleachers were the only remotely cool thing on this muggy mid-April afternoon. Ruin Bayou, Louisiana, had its nicer points, but an agreeable climate wasn't one. Fanning herself with the parent information sheet the coach's wife had distributed to all team hopefuls, Brynn tried shifting to a more comfy position—no easy feat at eight-months pregnant.

"Relax," her friend Vivian urged.

"Easy for you to say. Dom not only hits home runs, but sinks soccer goals and makes touchdowns—and that's all before breakfast. Meanwhile, poor Cayden…" Brynn cupped her bulging belly as her son tripped on his way to home plate. "Well, let's just say when it comes to athletic talent, he unfortunately inherited my family genes."

"Stop. Little Cayden's just going through a rough patch. Losing his dad like that…" She added a few clucks to her shaking head.

As was usually the case when recalling Mack's untimely demise, Brynn threw up a little in her mouth.

When Cayden looked to her for reassurance, Brynn blew him a kiss. He might be trying out for a *big boy* team, but he'd never be too old for some good, old-fashioned mommy sugar.

As the pitcher wound up for his throw, Brynn's stomach churned. *Please, please, please,* she prayed to her disaster of a dead husband, who had also happened to be one of the most celebrated hitters to ever come out of the state. *If you ever had so much as a shred of decency in you, send your sweet son a smidge of your batting skill...*

"Strike one!"

Not only had Cayden missed the ball, but he'd cowered when it came near him. Having grown up watching his dad play from a box seat in Busch Stadium III, Cayden had worshipped the man and the game, literally wearing a Cardinals baseball cap nearly every day since he'd been born. Any sane person would've thought Mack spent his free time playing catch with his son, but nothing could be further from the truth.

The pitcher threw again.

"Strike two!"

This time, Cayden had ducked to avoid the ball.

Vivian let loose with a low wolf whistle. "Who is that?"

Brynn's gaze drifted to where her friend pointed. A giant of a man strode to the outfield, kneeling to talk to a pint-size player. His faded jeans, white T-shirt and Geaux Saints baseball cap didn't mask hard-edged masculinity. A certain larger-than-life, take-charge essence emanated from the man even as he had a simple conversation with a child. The way the man leaned in, seemed to genuinely listen to whatever the distraught child had on his mind, told a different story from the guy's tough outer shell. His body language said he cared like a father, but Brynn was familiar with most of the little league crowd and was sure she'd have remembered a dad who looked like him.

"Whew…" Vivian was also using her info packet as a fan. "What I wouldn't give to be single right about now."

"Excuse me?" Sean, Vivian's husband, nudged her shoulder. "I'm sitting right here."

"Oh, yeah." She apologized with a kiss. "Looking at that hunk, I temporarily forgot."

Brynn fought not to roll her eyes. Vivian had it all. A great husband who adored her and a perfect son and home. She had everything Brynn had once taken for granted, but now knew she'd never have again.

The pitcher wound up for Cayden's third and final try as he'd already had four other turns and failed to hit a single pitch. In the span of a heartbeat, the ball flashed straight for her son, only to clang the chain-link fence behind him.

"Strike three! You're out!"

As he scuffed his little sneakered feet off the field, Cayden dropped his chin to his chest. Brynn's heart ached for him. Why, at this age, did Ruin Bayou's team have to be about competition? Why couldn't it be purely about fun and learning good sportsmanship? Once Cayden was old enough to learn the facts about his father, he'd receive harsh truths no child should ever learn. Until then, Brynn wanted to shelter him and hold him close. She'd tried a dozen times to talk him out of even going for this team, but he'd insisted.

He'd been so despondent ever since Mack's death, Brynn hoped maybe for once luck would be on his side.

"He gave it a good try…" Brynn resented Vivian's

stab at comfort when she slipped her arm around her for a supportive squeeze. "He's a full year younger than a lot of these other boys. You wait and see, next year at this time, Cayden's going to set this field on fire."

"Give it a rest," Sean said to his wife. "Coach hasn't even posted the team yet. Let's not count Cayden out until this is official."

Though Sean's words were kind, Brynn wasn't delusional. Boy after boy strode to home base, swinging and hitting for all they were worth. Six home runs had been made. Twelve triples. Not only didn't her son make a single hit, but no catches.

When tryouts were over, the coach, surrounded by players and parents, called the numbers of the kids who'd made that season's Ruin Bayou Mud Bugs.

Cayden's number wasn't called.

While around him, his friends gave each other high fives, Cayden's eyes welled and lower lip trembled.

Brynn took his hand, leading him away from the crowd. "You did a great job, sweetie. Your dad would be proud."

"No, he wouldn't." Her son kicked the dirt in the parking lot. "I'm a loser. Dad hated losers. That's why he left us. He hated me."

Stopping short of their SUV, Brynn knelt in front of her son. "Don't you *ever* say that about yourself again," she said fiercely. "Baseball is just a stupid game, you hear me? Life is about much more. Your dad—"

"Baseball isn't stupid!" Cayden cried, pitching his bat and glove on the ground. "You are!"

Brynn reached for him, trying to grab the red T-shirt that had been so thoughtfully provided in return for the Mud Bug's fifty-dollar tryout fee, but he was too fast. He took off across a weed-choked field.

She started after him, but a male voice behind her called, "Let him go. He'll be all right."

Brynn turned to find the man she'd seen earlier in the outfield. Up close and personal, he was as intimidating as he was impressive. He'd also inserted himself smack in the middle of an intensely personal conversation to which he hadn't been invited. "If you don't mind, I'll be the judge of what's best for my son."

"By all means." The stranger held up his hands. Hyper kids and their parents made their way to their cars. An audience compounded the awkward factor. "Sorry. Last thing I want is to get into your family business, but I remember the sting of being cut from my grade-school team. Only by my senior year, I'd filled out a little and we went on to win the AA State Championship."

Mack had been on that team. Had this man known her husband?

"Anyway," he went on to say, "your boy might think this is the end of his world, but he'll turn out okay."

With everything in her, Brynn fought a flippant comeback. This stranger had no idea what Cayden had already been through—not to mention the baseball legend he'd had for a father. It was a cruel twist of fate that a sporting talent that should've come to the boy as naturally as breathing had escaped him.

"Thanks for your insight," Brynn muttered, "but instead of letting my six-year-old run away, I'd rather handle this loss by the traditional mom method—with plenty of ice cream and hugs."

"Sure." Hands tucked in his jeans pockets, the guy backed off. "And for the record—I never said either of those things were bad." Then as abruptly as he'd appeared, the stranger melded into the crowd.

Brynn was again alone, worrying about her son, only she now carried the additional burden of being embarrassed by her snippy attitude toward someone who was undoubtedly a friend of a friend and had meant well. She never used to be this angry, bitter shell of a woman, but then Cayden never used to run off crying, either.

Glad she'd worn jeans with sneakers, Brynn chased after her son as quickly as her pregnant belly allowed. "Cayden! Come here, sweetie!"

"Leave me alone!"

The closer she got, the deeper into the boggy woods he ran.

With sunlight fading, Brynn's stomach knotted. Not only were the woods home to whining mosquitoes, ticks and other biting bugs, but poisonous snakes and gators. "Cayden, sweetie, I know you're upset, but this is getting dangerous."

"Go away! I wanna be alone!"

Brynn wasn't especially prone to panic, but she honestly was at a loss as to what to do. Hands to her temples, she urged her mind to think and her pulse to slow. Her single-parenting books frowned on rewarding a child's poor behavior, but it wasn't as if Cayden had run off with malice in his heart. He was understandably hurt that his friends had the God-given skills to play baseball and not him.

The ground squished beneath her rubber soles and the air smelled dank. Darkness was closing in, accompanied by a cacophony of foreign sounds. Though the ballpark wasn't that far behind them, they might as well have been in a different world.

"Cayden, please, come here!" she called. "This isn't funny!"

When he failed to answer, her blood ran cold.

Anything could've happened.

Brynn now trekked through sloppy mud, making her footing treacherous. The vegetation was dense, choked with brambles and vines.

"Cayden! Answer me!"

Still nothing.

If something happened to her son, Brynn wasn't sure how she'd survive. Aside from a smattering of friends, she had no one. Prescandal, at the height of his fame, it'd seemed she and Mack were never alone. They'd been the golden couple everyone wanted to be with. Postscandal, she'd become a pariah. Assets frozen and beyond broke. If it hadn't been for Mack outright owning his old family home, Brynn and Cayden wouldn't even have a roof over their heads.

"Cayden!" Deeper and deeper into the now dark woods Brynn crept.

"Mommy…" His voice barely carried.

"Sweetie, call me again so I can find you!"

She heard her son, but also a low, guttural grunt.

Panic set in and the faster she tried reaching her son, the tougher time she had finding solid footing. Her feet and the hems of her maternity jeans were cold-soaked, yet her upper body was sticky with sweat. The stench of rotting leaves turned her stomach. The humidity was as unbearable as her storming pulse.

"I'm scared…"

"I know, angel." She trudged forward. "Do I sound closer?"

"I don't know."

Foliage clawed at Brynn, making her every move torture. The grunt came again, filling her mind's eye with horrific images of her baby boy clamped between an alligator's jaws.

"Mommy, please hurry! It's gonna eat me!"

Panic surged through Brynn, making her strong but stupid, chasing after her boy without a clue where to find him.

"Thanks for helping me out."

"Anytime, man. Looks like you're going to have a great team." Tristan Bartoni shook Jason's hand. They'd been friends since Mrs. Fleck sat them next to each other in the second grade. A week later, he remembered with a chuckle, she'd separated them for talking too much.

"What's caught your funny bone?" Jason hefted the last of the equipment into his truck bed. The vehicle had come along with his recent election win as Ruin Bayou Chief of Police. Not only was the rig equipped with flashing lights and a siren, but tires that could handle damn near any terrain—a good thing considering the whole town was practically a swamp. His wife and toddler son had already long since gone home.

"Just thinking how much trouble we used to get in. Hard to believe where we are now."

Jason snorted. "Yeah. Back when we used to sit in detention every afternoon, who'd have thought we'd now be in charge?" He elbowed Tristan. "Well, me anyway. I don't know what you fancy navy SEALs do."

"Yeah, yeah." Tristan took out the keys to his own more modest black Ford pickup. "Just keep tellin' yourself that. You might keep Ruin Bayou safe, but my jurisdiction's the world."

"Modest much?" Jason had climbed behind his wheel.

"Nah." Tristan slipped his key into the ignition when he noticed the SUV the crabby pregnant woman had stood alongside was still parked at the far end of the lot, only with no one inside. She hadn't chased after her kid

on her own, had she? Mother Nature was a full-on rav-
ing bitch in these parts. "Hold up a minute. We might
have a situation..."

CAYDEN LOVED HIS MOM A WHOLE, big bunch, but right
now he wanted his dad. His mom said his dad died, but
most times Cayden wasn't even sure what that meant.
All he really knew was that his dad was gone and ever
since they left their house in St. Louis, all his mom ever
did was cry.

Now he was stuck up in a tree and his big toe hurt
really bad and he was pretty sure something giant was
trying to eat him.

"Mommy!"

He barely heard her say, "I'm coming, sweetie!"

He usually hated it when his mom called him sweetie
pie and stuff like he was a little kid, but out here, it was
kind of nice, knowing how much she loved him. He worried once the baby came, she'd only love his new sister,
then he'd be all alone.

Cayden started to cry, and he hated crying.

Crying was for stupid babies.

He called out for her again and again, but this time,
heard nothing. Forever and ever he sat alone in the tree,
until even his own breathing sounded scary.

"Cayden?" Who was that? Sounded like Coach
Jason. *"Mrs. Langtoine?"* Was he coming to tell him
he made the team?

Light bounced through the dark trees, making everything look *waaaay* more spookier. "Coach? I'm up
here! All my bones are broke bad! And there's an alligator trying to eat me!"

"You mean this guy?" Coach held up a loud-
mouthed frog.

"Guess it could've been him."

Coach asked, "Where's your mom?"

"Don't know. I—I think she's lost."

FROM DEEP WITHIN THE WOODS, Brynn glanced over her shoulder and saw a light bobbing in the gloom. Not sure if her eyes were playing tricks on her, she did a double take. "Hello?"

A hulking figure emerged from the brush. "Mrs. Langtoine?"

"You…" The man she'd admired on the field for his knack for talking with the players and whom she'd later regretted snapping at for sharing his advice concerning her son had now come to her rescue. Relief sagging her shoulders, she cupped her hands to her belly.

He extended his hand. "High time for a formal introduction. Tristan Bartoni. Guess I owe you an apology. Seems letting your boy run off wasn't such a great idea."

"Brynn Langtoine. And actually, if I'd done as you suggested and left him alone instead of chasing him, he probably wouldn't have gone so far." The man's fingers enveloped hers. His height and breadth made her feel all at once vulnerable, yet strangely safe. "Have you seen my son? I thought I had him, but this swamp got me all turned around. Sounds don't carry right, and…" She shook her head. "I need to find Cayden. He's all I have."

"Understood." Tristan punched numbers into an electronic gadget, then took a handheld radio from a side pocket in his cargo pants. Into the radio, he said, "I've got the mom. How's it going with the boy?"

"Got him," came a static-garbled voice.

Relief turned Brynn's knees to rubber. When she nearly collapsed, her new friend was there to support her. "Whoa. We've had enough excitement for tonight.

"Copy that," he said into his radio. "Meet up back at the trucks." With the radio returned to its pocket, he again consulted his gadget. "You hauled ass through rough terrain."

"Um, thanks, I guess." Legs again steady beneath her, Brynn straightened, trying to regain her composure. "Desperation makes a body do crazy things."

"No kidding. Now we have to trek damn near two miles to get back."

"Sorry."

"Oh, hey—" he held back an armful of brush for her to pass "—I'm not complaining. Truth is, you're doing me a favor. This beats the hell out of watching reality TV. Been cooped up at my mom's too long."

"Oh?" She wanted to ask why, but figured not only wasn't it her business, but the last thing she needed was to form a connection with someone when it would inevitably fail. Since moving to Ruin Bayou just after Christmas, Brynn had done a good job of keeping to herself. Selling Mack's Escalade had given her enough cash to buy a less expensive SUV, and not have to get a job right away. But with that money dwindling, she couldn't hide forever.

Maybe not forever, her wounded heart cried, but at least until she had her baby.

After ten minutes walking in silence, he said, "I grew up around here and only knew one Langtoine. My mom said Mack's widow was back with their little boy. You her?"

"Yep." So much for hiding.

Chapter Two

Last thing Tristan wanted was to get in Brynn's business. He knew all too well what it was like to be caught in a situation bigger than he could handle. That said, he'd considered Mack a friend, and had been shocked and saddened by the allegations lodged against him.

The muck they sloshed through sucked at the soles of his boots, making travel arduous. Most women he'd encountered would've bitched a blue streak over being caught in this kind of mess, but Brynn trekked on without complaint.

"Go ahead," she said with a defensive tone, "ask away about my husband. Everyone else does." She stopped, tilting her head back, giving her long curls a shake before arranging them into a messy ponytail with a band she'd had on her wrist.

"Well?" Tristan probed. "Did he do it?"

"Which of his transgressions in particular? Gambling ring—check. Game fixing, partnership in an underground casino—check, check." She started walking.

Tristan whistled.

"That about sums it up."

And here I thought I'd had it bad. Sidestepping a log, he said, "Hang to the left just a bit."

She set a quicker pace than he'd expected from a

woman in her condition as she asked, "What's your story?"

"Complicated." And it still stung plenty bad. But he didn't discuss his past even with his mom, let alone a stranger. "Mack was a great guy. I can't imagine him—"

"You don't have to imagine it. I lived it." Her snippy voice had returned with a vengeance—not that he could blame her for being cranky.

"Back in school, Mack never even cheated on tests."

"And you did?" They kept an even pace and the look she cast his way wasn't exactly complimentary.

"Maybe once or twice in a pinch. Who didn't?"

"Me." He didn't appreciate her high-and-mighty tone. "And just think what that says about your moral character."

"Give me a break. I was thirteen."

Having reached a small creek, she said, "I don't remember crossing this before. Check your navigation thingy and make sure we're still going the right way."

"Seriously?" He shook his head. "I'm not the one needing to be rescued. And as for cheating, now that I think about it, I only did it once—on my Algebra midterm. But for the record, I felt so bad about it I went home and learned the work inside and out. Plus, the kid I copied off of made a lousy grade, so I didn't even reap any benefits." Lord, listen to him—rambling like a guilty third-grader. Why? What was it about Brynn that made him even care what she thought?

"MOMMY!" TEARS CAUGHT IN Brynn's throat when Cayden ran across the field to meet her, crushing her in a hug. Only two hours had passed since she'd last seen him, but it felt like a lifetime. "I was so scared."

"I know, baby." She kissed the top of his head. "Me, too."

"Coach Jason said I was really brave, and if I practice I might be able to play later in the summer with the team."

"That's awesome." Still holding her son, she looked to the man she also knew was the town police chief. "I can't thank you enough for your help. Tristan, you, too."

The man she'd spent a large portion of her evening with merely nodded.

The chief's truck radio squawked, then a dispatcher called him. "Looks like I'm needed down at the Suds & Swirl, but, Cayden, no more running off when things get rough, okay?"

In the truck light's glare, her little boy nodded.

"Promise?"

"Yeah," Cayden said with a solemn nod.

"All right, then." After a quick ruffle of Cayden's hair, Jason said, "Tristan, you got this handled?"

"You know it."

"Y'all have a good night, then."

Brynn thanked him again for his help finding her son, waving him on his way.

When Cayden climbed into their SUV's passenger side, she found herself once more on her own with Tristan. Immersed in darkness tempered only by the faint light of the moon, she wasn't sure what to do with her hands, let alone her galloping pulse. She owed him so much, and wanted to express her gratitude, but she was broken, and couldn't find words to match the emotion swelling in her heart. "What you did—and the coach—helping Cayden and I…" Rather than meet his intense dark gaze she looked to her clasped hands. "Well, I appreciate your help. I haven't had a lot of folks on my side lately, and—" Her voice cracked and that chink in her carefully constructed armor proved her undoing.

"Hey…" He approached her, but held a respectful distance.

She softly cried, covering her face with her hands. "What's wrong with me? Tonight could've turned out so bad, but for once, luck shone on me. I've been so strong, keeping everything in."

"Know the feeling," he said. "The stuff I went through with my ex-wife…" Jaw clenched, he shook his head. "Hell, I've been shot and had it hurt less."

"Can't say I've ever been shot." She managed a smile through her tears. "But my husband was, so I have known pain. The gambling and game-fixing were humiliating, but seeing Mack killed…" Her voice had turned raspy with grief.

"Mom!" Cayden popped his head out the open car window. "I'm hungry!"

"Duty calls." Brynn smiled and genuinely felt it. Which made her sad for having earlier been snarky and standoffish. Tristan seemed like a great guy. She needed to remember that not every man was as despicable as her ex.

"Where have you been?"

Tristan tried sneaking into his mom's house, but as he'd feared, the second the screen door creaked open, she was up from what she called her comfy crafting chair and paused the living room TV on one of her favorite shows.

In the kitchen, Donna grabbed two beers. He expected her to hand him one, but she kept them both for herself. "You've worried me to drink."

"Sorry." He rummaged through the fridge for his

own adult beverage. "After tryouts, one of the boys who didn't make it ran off into Lee Bayou. Jason tracked him, and I went after his mother."

"Oh?" Always on the hunt for a future daughter-in-law, her eyebrows shot up. "Anyone I know?"

He popped the top on his beer, taking a nice, long drink. "For this, you might want to sit down."

"I'm intrigued..." So much so that she fished through the pantry for a bag of chips.

"Whoa—thought your doctor told you to drop a few pounds?"

She fished out a handful, popping them into her mouth. "What he doesn't know won't hurt him."

Rolling his eyes, Tristan took her second beer and returned it to the fridge but let her keep her chips. "I already lost Dad to a heart attack. If you don't mind, I'd prefer keeping you."

After sticking out her tongue, she snagged a few more chips before closing the bag. "All right, enough lecturing. Tell me about your mystery date."

"It wasn't a date, but we had to rescue Mack's wife and son."

"Mack Langtoine?"

"Yep." Tristan needed another drink. Just as he never would've believed Andrea would leave him, he felt the same of his old friend cheating in the game he loved.

"What do you think of the whole thing? Was he guilty?"

He shrugged. "Brynn seems to think so."

"Poor girl." His mom drank more beer. "And then to have him gunned down like that, right in front of her. Too much for a tiny thing like her to bear—especially being pregnant."

Joining her at the table, he asked, "How far along is she?"

"Garden club gossip has her at eight months."

"So she's in your club?"

"I wish." She fingered the bag of chips. "Judging by what she's already done with the old Langtoine place's yard, she's got a green thumb, but very much keeps to herself. Her neighbor to the east is Georgia Booth. She's been over three times with muffins and Brynn never even answers the door. Georgia didn't think it proper, and had to practically stalk her outside to even bring the girl baked goods. Peculiar, if you ask me."

Tristan had another view. "What if Brynn's scared? So many people have trash-talked her, associating her with Mack's crimes, she's probably terrified of being judged."

"That's pretty deep," his mom observed. "Since when are you so smart?"

He laughed. "Know what they say about with hindsight comes twenty-twenty vision? Well, if there's anything I've learned from my divorce, it's that when it comes to relationships, like Brynn, I should be afraid— very afraid."

"Hurry, sweetie." Brynn gave Cayden's behind a light smack as he raced back upstairs for his forgotten book bag.

Her smile faded as she remembered the panic from the night before. Cayden had been concerned about not earning a spot on the baseball team, but if he'd been hurt in that swamp, she'd have lost so much more.

And yet, for all the spooky growls and grunts she'd heard, nothing had hurt them—in large part due to Tristan and his friend Jason. The last position she'd ever wanted to be in was finding herself depending on another man, but for those couple hours it'd taken Tristan to lead her back to civilization, that's exactly what circumstance had forced her to do. And look at her—still in one piece. All limbs intact.

Strangest fact of all, she had the oddest craving to see Tristan again. To properly thank him.

"Found it, Mom." Book bag in hand, Cayden raced down the stairs. "Let's hurry. I have to be extra early. It's my turn to feed Toby." Toby was the classroom turtle. Feeding him was a great honor.

Driving her son to school, Brynn tried remembering times she'd been as excited. Nearly every one of Mack's games. Seated with the other wives, she'd been so proud of her man. Prouder still of her little boy and of finally being accepted into the *popular* crowd. Her father, an East Coast fisherman, had died at sea. Her mother, not a year after, had passed of what the aunt who'd raised her diagnosed as a broken heart. Brynn hadn't been much older than Cayden, and at times, she'd thought the pain more than she could bear. But she had. And she'd grown and done well enough in school to earn a full ride to Notre Dame—a magical place so far from all she'd ever known, she'd been convinced only magic could be found within those creamy-colored brick walls.

When she not only met and fell in love with Mack, but discovered the sheer joy of having him love her, too, never had she felt more complete.

"Mom?"

"Uh-huh?" She stopped for the light on Elm.

"Why didn't Dad rescue us last night?"

Her stomach knotted, and she searched for just the right thing to say. No matter how many times she told Cayden his father was gone, he hadn't fully absorbed the fact. He was still convinced Mack would appear. As if he'd only been gone on an extended series of away games.

She accelerated when the light turned green. "Sweetie, you know why. More than anything, I know he'd never have wanted anything bad to happen to you—either one of us. But remember when we talked about how he isn't coming back?"

Chin to his chest, Cayden said, "I thought you might not've really meant it. Like when we order pizza and you tell me you're so full you're never eating again."

Pulling up to the curb in front of the town's only elementary school, Brynn searched for words when there were none. "I wish it was like that. I really do."

He unfastened his seat belt, grabbed his bag from the floorboard, then hopped out of the car.

"Where's my kiss?" she asked.

He blanched. "It's bad enough I didn't make the team. I can't kiss my mom in front of my friends."

That comment set the tone for her day....

A THUNDERSTORM IN THE NIGHT had cleared the humidity, making for a gorgeous morning. As Tristan was on indefinite leave until he got his head back in what his commanding officer deemed a *good place,* he split his time between missing his kid, wondering what he might've done differently with his ex and working out.

Before the heat grew too bad, he figured he might as well get a jump start on at least one out of three.

His usual run took him down Mulberry Lane to Herring Park Trail. But something his mom had mentioned about Brynn Langtoine stuck in his head. That bit about her having a green thumb. Considering the fact that his mom and at least half the other gardening fanatics on their block had already been outside for hours, he figured it was a safe bet Brynn might already be working in her beds, as well.

Mack and his family hadn't lived far. A half mile at most, at the end of a quiet cul-de-sac.

In just over four minutes, Tristan reached the simple two-story home. The front porch and an upper balcony were trimmed in black wrought-iron, reminding him of childhood trips to New Orleans. When they'd been high school juniors, Mack's folks had gone out of town to visit his grandparents. Mack had thrown a party and midway through the keg, a few of the looser girls in their class had stood on that balcony, flashing the guys for Mardi Gras beads. Not long after, the Langtoine's nosy neighbor, Georgia Booth, called the cops and the festivities had been shut down.

In front of the house, Tristan slowed his pace to barely a jog, striving to get a look in the backyard without being too obvious. Only it turned out he'd been right in his assumption Brynn would be out on such a fine day.

He got caught.

"Take a picture," she called upon catching him staring. "It'll last longer."

"Guilty as charged." Out of breath and laughing, he paused by the birdbath Mack gave his mother on her fortieth birthday. She'd died of cancer a couple years later. Mack had been playing ball for Notre Dame and his dad had taken off, never to be seen again. Mack's grandparents had owned the house and when they died, they left it to him. "Your boy—Cayden? Already at school?"

Gardening spade in hand, she rocked back on her heels. "It was his turn to clean the class turtle's tank and feed him. I took him in early."

"Figured as much."

"How so?" Sunlight slanted though Spanish moss-drizzled trees and there wasn't a breath of wind. The school bus's squeaky brakes could be heard at the corner of Hickory and Pine.

Grinning, Tristan said, "From my own days at Ruin Bayou High, I figure any kid on this street has about three and a half minutes to hustle to the front of his house. Plenty of time to grab a Pop-Tart or play a quick game of fetch with your dog. Meaning, if Cayden hadn't left early, he'd still be here, horsing around."

"You're good," she noted when sure enough, right on schedule, the bus screeched to a stop. Even from the backyard, the sound of kids bickering, stealing sack lunches and pulling pigtails carried on the morning's still air. Soon, the rolling riot moved on, returning peace to Cherry Court until retracing the route at 3:25.

"I've been hustling Cayden out to catch the bus for over five months, but I've never timed it quite like that."

Though he shrugged, the SEAL in Tristan was glad not to have lost his flair for efficiency. Also in his personal skill arsenal was being observant, which was how he came to notice an intimidating pile of redwood planks, bolts and faux wood-colored plastic roofs, slides and swing seats. The pirate-type fort was pretty cool—at least it would be once it was assembled. Any kid would love it. Which made him think of his own son, Jack. The one topic he worked hard to avoid.

Trying to focus on the ungodly mess of materials rather than thoughts of how Jack was spending his morning, Tristan was startled to look up and find Brynn standing next to him. Sure, he'd seen her at the ballpark, but in fading light and then complete darkness, he hadn't really *seen* her.

Since she'd squeezed her considerable assets into a

figure-hugging Cardinals T-shirt rather than a loose maternity top, he noted she was barely five foot tall with a mess of curly ginger hair and a baby bump the size of two watermelons. Barefoot, wearing a long, gauzy skirt, she pressed her hands to the small of her back. He wondered if her back was hurting. If so, he was sure she'd never admit it. Backlit by morning sun, her skirt turned transparent. It took a ton of willpower to keep his gaze from dropping to her shapely legs.

"Big mess, huh?" She nodded toward the unassembled fort. "Cayden's had a tough time of it lately. Thought for his birthday, this might perk him up. D-Shawn's Lumber wanted an extra five hundred for assembly, but I figured on saving the money by doing it myself. How hard can it be, you know?" She faintly smiled and damn if Tristan didn't find himself caught up in her world, smiling and nodding right along.

"Um, yeah." Unsure what to do with his hands, he rammed them in his pockets.

When she cocked her head, corkscrew curls tumbled over her shoulder. She was so pretty it rendered him stupid. Before he could stop the words from spilling from his mouth, he said, "Want help? With Cayden's gift? I'm fairly decent with tools." Listen to him—practically begging her to let him spend hours in her backyard. The whole point of Tristan being on leave back home in Louisiana was to escape the pain of losing his son to a different time zone. Last thing he needed was getting wrangled into what could turn into a multiday project. Worse yet, would be the proximity of being around another man's child.

Another man's wife. Even if the man was dead.

Say no, his gut silently pleaded to Brynn. As long as she turned down his offer, Tristan had nothing to fear.

Then she nodded her pretty head. "Never thought I'd hear myself say this, but honestly, if I'm going to have a prayer of finishing by Cayden's birthday, I'd very much appreciate your help."

Chapter Three

The moment the words left her mouth, Brynn regretted them. What had she been thinking? If she didn't want new friends period, she certainly didn't need one as attractive as Tristan. In the bright light of day, square jaw sporting sexy stubble and dark eyes hidden by mirrored aviator sunglasses, he not only towered over her, but reminded her how amazing it'd felt when he'd charged to her rescue—only she wasn't in the market for a shining knight.

She'd once cast Mack in that role and look how disastrously that had turned out.

"Forgive me," she backpedaled. "I didn't mean to stick you with my mess. You were only being polite when you offered, so please don't think I expect you to—"

"No," he insisted, "I want to help. Cayden seems like a great kid. After not making the team with the rest of his friends, he deserves some fun."

"Yeah, but that fun is going to come at too big a price to you. Really, I can handle the fort on my own." Her huge belly made it a struggle for her to even pick up the rest of her gardening tools. Common sense dictated she may not want Tristan's help, but she sure needed it.

When she barely made it upright without his hand on

her arm holding her steady, he lowered his sunglasses to meet her gaze. "With all due respect, as big as you are, I'm not sure you're even going to make it back into the house under your own steam."

"Thanks." It took a ton of self-restraint not to childishly stick out her tongue.

"Hey, I happen to think baby bumps are cute."

"Uh-huh." As long as she kept reminding herself she was no more in the market for romance than he was, they'd get along just fine.

"SORRY TO NOT HAVE SOMETHING fancier."

"I'm so hungry, cardboard would taste good," Tristan said when Brynn approached bearing a plate filled with two egg salad sandwiches, chips and a pickle. In the four hours he'd been working, Tristan had already assembled the fort's exterior frame. He'd worked up one hell of an appetite. He downed the better half of his first sandwich in a couple bites before remembering he wasn't with his SEAL buddies, Deacon, Garrett and Calder. "Jeez, sorry." He used the napkin she'd also given him. "I do have manners—I just don't usually have a whole lot of cause for using them."

"You're fine," she said with a shy smile. "Mack was the same after a long day of games."

Setting the plate she'd given him on the raised fort's floor, he said, "That must've been a rush, huh? Him playing for the Cards?"

"It really was…" Judging by the way her smile faded, he'd touched on a sensitive issue.

He finished his second sandwich. "Never mind. None of my business."

"No, it's okay. Just hurts, you know? Remembering the good times. In a twisted way, it's almost easier dwelling on the bad."

True. When he thought of what a great little family he used to have, it killed him. Now with his ex remarried and his son in California, he preferred thinking how much he despised her instead of how much he missed his kid. While they'd been divorced for three years, she and Jack had always lived close. It'd been barely over a month since she'd sprung her marriage and cross-country move on him. The news shook him to the point that on his last mission, his concentration had been off while leading his team through a mine field. Damn near got them all killed. Once they were safely home, his CO hadn't minced words about what a "shit storm" Tristan's recent job performance had been. When the man whom Tristan greatly respected urged him to take time off, Tristan agreed.

"I had just found out I was pregnant when everything fell apart. The scandals only fully erupted after he was killed." Leaning against the fort's redwood frame, she turned reflective. "It was as if some higher power flipped a switch. One day, my life was intact. The next, it was gone."

Exactly how he'd felt when Andrea took off.

After a few moments' shared silence while he finished his lunch, she said, "Some days I have to force myself out of bed. For Cayden, and this little one," she added with a pat to her belly. "I can't just give up."

"You're lucky you have Cayden—and the baby." He grabbed the cordless drill he'd brought along with an assortment of other tools from his house. He could've fought Andrea for joint custody, but figured in the end, it'd be harder for Jack.

The arrangement was pretty new, but he now only

saw his son a couple times a year. Nowhere near enough. As much as it killed Tristan to admit, aside from him cabbaging on to his family, Jack's stepfather was all right. An engineer. Worked nine to five and provided a more stable home life than Tristan ever could.

"You said you were in the navy, but never mentioned what you do."

"I'm a SEAL."

"For real?" She choked on a laugh.

He screwed in a support joist. "Why's that so hard to believe?"

She twirled a dandelion she'd plucked from the yard. "Guess I never believed they existed outside of movies."

"Yet you were married to a major league baseball player?"

Grinning up at him, she said, "I've met a hundred of those. Never met one SEAL."

THE SECOND CAYDEN JUMPED OFF the school bus's big bottom step, he ran across the front yard and into the house.

He dumped his book bag at the base of the stairs. "Mom!"

He ran calling from room to room, but didn't find her—not even in the kitchen or bathroom.

She wasn't dead, was she?

Ever since his dad died, he wondered what kept all of the other grown-ups alive. What if they all croaked? Who would make dinner and help with his baths and homework and tuck him into bed?

He dragged a chair from the kitchen table over to the counter where his mom kept the cookie jar. Climbing onto what his mom had called butcher-block wood, he grabbed three oatmeal cookies from the pig-shaped jar. He wished for chocolate chip, but ever since Mom said his baby sister was growing inside her, they had to be real healthy. That just made him hate his sister more.

The window over the kitchen sink was open.

A funny sound came from the backyard.

Still on the counter, he scooted to where he could see out the window and what he found almost made him fall. That big guy who'd saved his mom from the alligators was building his birthday fort!

Careful not to break his cookies, he grabbed one of his favorite Scooby-Doo granola bars from the cabinet and rolled onto his belly to get down, bumping open the back screen door with his butt. "Mom! It's awesome!"

"Hey, sweetie." When she gave him a big hug, he was so glad she wasn't dead that he didn't even squirm. "Remember Mr. Tristan from last night?"

"I don't think we officially met." The man held out his hand for Cayden to shake just like Cayden was a grown-up.

"Nice to meet you." Cayden liked it when grownups didn't treat him like a kid. He was getting awfully old. And once he had his birthday on Saturday he'd be seven. That was like *super* old. "Thank you for working on my fort. Mom kept saying she was gonna, but my baby sister makes her too tired."

"You're having a girl?" the big man—Tristan—said to Cayden's mom. He had a kinda funny smile.

Cayden's mom smiled, too. "I'm having a devil of a time coming up with a pretty name. Cayden, here, is supposed to be helping. But so far, all he's come up with are Bug Guts Langtoine, Monkey Ears or Donkey Butt." Wrinkling her nose, his mom said, "Not sure I like any of those."

"I don't know…" Tristan winked at Cayden. "I like

Monkey Ears. Everyone knows all babies have them. My little sister does."

"You have a sister?" Cayden and his mom asked at the same time.

She laughed.

So did Tristan. "I do. Her name's Franny Newton. Once she married Mr. Newton, I started calling her Fig Newton. She's a music teacher and lives all the way in Iowa with my brother-in-law, two nieces and nephew. My mom's going to visit her in a few weeks." He lowered his voice to a whisper. "But my sister's an awful cook, so I try not to go unless my mom makes me. Or, unless I have lots of Scooby-Doo granola bars like you have there."

"You eat these, too?" Cayden laughed. "They're for kids!"

"When I was a kid, I used to love Scooby-Doo."

"That's cool! But hey, we've got lots to eat besides granola bars. My mom's a super good cooker. Wanna stay for dinner? She makes the best meat loaf in the whole, wide world!"

The grown-ups looked kind of funny at each other, then Tristan said, "Thanks. But I should get home to do my chores."

"WHAT'S WRONG?" BRYNN ASKED Cayden after Tristan had left.

While she sat at one end of the table, snapping green beans, he sat at the other, completing his handwriting homework.

"I couldn't get you to stop talking when we were outside, but now, you're not saying a word."

He shrugged.

"Is it because we're having fish for dinner instead

of meat loaf? I know you don't like it, but I'll make the homemade tartar sauce you love."

"Why didn't Tristan wanna stay for dinner? Is it because you cooked fish? Couldn't you have please made meat loaf? Then, I know he would've stayed."

"It's not that easy." Back aching, she stood, rinsing the beans at the sink before slipping them into the pan of water she'd already put on the stove to boil.

"Sure it is." He put down his chubby pencil. "What's the matter? Doesn't he like me?"

"Sweetie, of course, he likes you." She pressed a kiss to the top of his head. "Everyone loves you."

"Not the baseball team."

"That's different," she said, although to a kid, she could see how the issue might be confusing.

"Nobody loves me," he cried. "Not Coach Jason or Tristan or especially Dad!"

When he ran off toward the stairs, clomping up to his room, Brynn knew she should've followed, but truthfully, she was too exhausted.

ONCE AGAIN, THOUGH TRISTAN wanted nothing to do with kids, as they only reminded him of Jack, that night he found himself back at the ballpark, surrounded.

He'd helped Jason set out the bases and chalk the field.

They now stood side by side while the team completed laps and circuit calisthenics. The sky was an angry, tumultuous gray, but the official rule book read if thunder was heard or lightning seen, then coaches stopped play. Since the guys needed practice, until the weather turned officially ugly, it was game on.

Jason leaned against the trunk of the big oak that'd been growing in the outfield for so long no one had the heart to cut it. "Town gossip says you spent the afternoon with Mack's widow, building a fort for his little boy."

"Knew there was a reason I ran from this busybody town soon as I got my diploma." Tristan pulled his ball cap lower on his forehead.

"Looking for love in all the wrong places?"

"Hell, no," he said to his supposed friend. "I was doing her and her kid a favor, that's all. Might've been nice if you'd done the same and just let him on your team."

"You know I couldn't do that. This is a traveling squad and logistically, I can't handle over twelve. Even with you as my assistant coach, I won't have near as much time as when I was a deputy. Usually, by mid-season, someone drops out. Who knows? Maybe we'll take him on then."

"Yeah, yeah…" Tristan said. "And I never told you I'd be your assistant coach."

"It's not like you've got anything better going on. Unless you'd rather hang out with your mom, making crafts for the rest home?"

Tristan fairly growled. "I'd rather be back in Virginia Beach, doing my job."

"And we both know until you get your head straight about losing Jack, that's not going to happen." After shouting at two slackers to pick up their pace, Tristan winced when Jason elbowed him. "Unless there's something you're not telling me? Like you prefer a certain pregnant redhead's company to mine?"

"Watch it," Tristan warned. Though he barely knew Brynn, out of respect for his old friend Mack, he wouldn't tolerate jokes involving her—even if they were at his expense.

"TRISTAN!"

The next morning, Brynn's heart ached to see Cayden run across the too-tall lawn to give their new friend a hug. With sun slanting through the trees, glistening in the dew, she should've been thrilled to find Tristan already in their yard, wielding his drill. Instead, she wished she'd never met him.

It didn't take a rocket scientist to see Cayden was desperately seeking a father figure and Tristan was his latest target.

Even if Brynn hadn't been practically fifteen months pregnant, and interested in him in more of a romantic light than as merely a friend, she assumed he'd soon be back on his Virginia Beach base. She'd also noticed his habit of never saying anything personal about himself. Why? Like Mack, did he have something to hide? Or also like her husband, did he just not trust her enough to share certain issues? Toss in the not-so-small fact that she'd lost her husband to a shooting and Tristan had dedicated his life to playing with guns?

Well, anyone could see they were hardly well suited.

Last night, long after Cayden had gone to sleep, she'd stayed up, nursing heartburn with decaffeinated peppermint tea. Burning curiosity led to her researching navy SEALs. The one thing she'd taken from a solid two hours of internet surfing was that statistically, SEALs suffered from a high rate of divorce—not to mention getting hurt.

Even if one day she chose to open her heart again, Tristan would be her worst possible match. She'd never tell him, but truthfully she didn't blame his wife for leaving. He'd no doubt been gone more than he was home. Only, he hadn't just been off playing ball in Sacramento, but risking his life in war-ravaged cesspools.

Right on cue, the school bus soon enough arrived on their street.

Cayden gave Tristan a final hug before dashing off toward his ride.

With her son gone, Brynn meandered over to where Tristan strong-armed one of the fort's plastic roofs into position. "Need help?"

"Thanks, but I've got it."

Shielding her eyes from the sun, she said, "At the rate you're going, you'll be done by this afternoon."

"Hope so. Cayden told me his party's Saturday. That's only two days away."

"Don't remind me." She groaned. "Between the added yard work and baking, I'm starting to regret the whole idea. Plus, he'll be seeing a lot of the boys who made the little league team."

After screwing the roof in place, he said, "I'll tackle the lawn."

"That's not what I meant. Please don't think I was fishing for a helping hand. You've already done too much."

He ignored her protests in favor of continuing to work. He seemed so driven, she felt as though she were an intruder in her own backyard. And then, he stopped. "Mind if I ask you a personal question?"

"Go for it." His expression seemed so serious, she almost smiled. Was Mr. Privacy finally going to open up? Even with his eyes narrowed and mouth set grim, he was still far too handsome for his own good—or maybe, that should be for her own good!

As if nervous, he tossed the lightweight cordless drill from hand to hand. "Like me, you had a crap marriage, right?"

"I guess…" Where in the world was he going?

"Well, last night a friend said I should date, but why? Guess my question for you is—in light of what you went through with Mack—do you feel the same? Like the train left the station on that whole part of your life?"

"You're amazing." Her knees nearly buckled from the shimmering relief of having a kindred spirit when it came to understanding the emotional pain of what Mack had put her through. "My friend Vivian is constantly hinting she's found the perfect guy to hook me up with. No matter how many times I tell her I'm never going to be interested, she refuses to listen."

A muscle popped on his square, whisker-covered jaw. "Amen."

She told herself the sudden lightness in her chest had nothing to do with Tristan, but in truth, it had everything to do with him. Before they'd met, she'd believed herself utterly alone when it came to her rejection of all matters having to do with the heart. "No one gets the fact that Cayden and my baby girl are all I'll ever need."

"I do," Tristan quietly said. "Although, at the rate your grass is growing, if you still don't want to take me up on my offer to mow, you're going to have a long, hot afternoon." When he blasted her with a slow, crooked grin, Brynn lost all power to deny him. What would it hurt for him to do her one, last favor?

"THAT'S JUST RIDICULOUS…" Vivian had parted the living-room curtains and sat practically salivating over Tristan mowing Brynn's yard wearing nothing but cargo shorts and leather flip-flops. "Outside of movies and magazines, I've never seen a man with a body that hard."

"Stop!" Brynn scolded in a stage whisper even though they were alone.

"Why? It's not like he can see or hear me. And besides, I might be married, but I'm not dead. If I were you, I'd be all over that."

Clearing her throat, Brynn pointed to her bulging belly. "Reality check? Even if I were in the market for a man, I get the impression Tristan's never going to be in the market for another woman."

"They all say that." Vivian finally lowered the curtain. "But just you wait. Before too long, I guarantee that man will be sniffing skirts just like the rest of them."

"Do you have to be so crude?" Brynn shifted positions so that Tristan and his amazing chest were out of view.

Vivian rolled her eyes. "Do you have to be such a prude?"

"Let's agree to disagree and work on the party." Consulting her list, Brynn asked, "Did you ever find the pony guy's number? I know it's short notice, but Cayden's been so upset about not making the team, I want this birthday to be extra special."

Back to ogling Tristan, Vivian said, "You do know the next town over—Boynton—has a noncompetitive team? I'm sure Cayden would be more than welcome to play with them."

Something about Vivian's tone set Brynn on edge. "Cayden wants to play with his friends."

"He'll make more." She'd again turned back from the window.

Brynn wasn't sure how to respond. Her aunt had raised her to always be polite, but this was one case when she'd like nothing more than to give Vivian a piece of her mind. "Hasn't your son ever wanted something, only not to get it? Cayden's already lost his home and father and friends in St. Louis. Would it kill you to show a smidge of compassion?"

Leaning forward, resting her elbows on her knees, Vivian said, "Okay, whoa. You took that completely wrong. All I meant was that if you really want Cayden to play ball on Ruin Bayou's competitive team, at the very least you'll need to invest in a private coach."

"Brynn, didn't you tell her?" Tristan stood in the open door, the full, muscular breadth of him blocking the light of the sun.

Mouth dry, pulse racing, Brynn asked, "T-tell her what?"

"That I'm Cayden's private coach. And by the time I get done helping him, he'll easily outhit any kid on that team."

Chapter Four

With Vivian thankfully gone, and Tristan and his mouth-watering chest in the front yard weed-eating, Brynn had finally gotten around to hanging her small family's clothes on the line. Mack's grandmother who'd lived in the home before her hadn't owned a dryer. In the winter, it'd sometimes been rough finding a warm enough sunny day, but now that she'd gotten the hang of living more simply, Brynn had started to like it.

In St. Louis, the housekeeper had done laundry. Here in Ruin Bayou, Brynn had grown to find pleasure in the simple comfort of handling her son's small clothes. She'd lost so much, but whenever she was tempted to abandon herself to pity, she remembered how many blessings she had left.

"Haven't seen a woman under seventy doing this in a while…" Tristan rounded the corner of the house, blasting her with his lopsided smile. If she asked politely, would it be wrong for her to request he put his T-shirt back on? "If you need a dryer, I'm sure Mom wouldn't mind you doing loads at our house. Or, I could help you haul it all to the Suds & Swirl."

"That's okay." She'd come to one of her bras and shoved it beneath a sheet. "But thanks for the offer."

"Sure." He folded his arms, which only exaggerated

the size of his forearms and biceps. Like Vivian had earlier observed, his body was indeed ridiculous.

"Um, thanks, too, for your help mowing. The yard looks great for Cayden's party."

"Sure. By this afternoon, I should also have the fort finished."

"You're amazing—doing all this for strangers." She pinned the first corner of the damp white sheet to the line. The fresh scents of laundry detergent and just-mown grass and the wholly masculine aroma of a man who'd spent hours working hard in the sun blended into an intoxicating balm that, had it been possible to bottle and sell, might've been called *Home*. Which only compounded the situation's awkward-factor.

Before she'd even found the sheet's other corner, Tristan already had it in hand, stretching it for her. "Let me."

"Tristan, stop." After placing a pin in the center and another near his hand, carefully avoiding even the briefest contact, Brynn shook her head. "You can't imagine how much I appreciate your help, but I've got this. I might look helpless, but I'm still getting around fine. The baby's not due for another month and that's far too long for me to spend every day lounging on the sofa."

Ignoring her request, he took a towel from the basket, folding it over the line before helping himself to her clothespin bag. "How was your pregnancy with Cayden?"

"Different." Her heart couldn't bear thinking of the exquisite nursery her little boy had had. The opulent, over-the-top showers. The private room in an exclusive VIP wing at a birthing center. Friends, servants and Mack, doting on her 24/7.

"I'll bet." He seemed as if he wanted to say more, but once again, didn't.

"It's a special time—at least it was for me with Cayden. This go around…" She shrugged, fighting back tears. Changing the subject was a must. "What you said when Vivian was here—about you helping Cayden with his baseball? I can't thank you enough for once again offering your help, but…" She shrugged.

"But let me guess—you can do it yourself?"

Steeling her grip on the wicker clothes basket, Brynn nodded. "I made the mistake of depending on Mack for essentially everything, and I'll never do it again. For my sake, for my children's, I can't."

He laughed, which only incensed her. "My personal life might be a mess right now, but if there's anything being in the navy has taught me, it's that you're always stronger surrounded by a well-oiled team." Grabbing his T-shirt from where he'd draped it over the back of a patio chair, he shrugged it on. "Something you might want to think about as you head into battle."

"I'm raising a little boy and will soon have a baby girl—that's love, not war."

He turned his back on her, sauntering toward Cayden's fort. "Not sure what planet you're living on, but pretty sure raising even one kid isn't for the faint of heart—I can't imagine what it's going to take for you to handle two."

TWO HOURS LATER, BRYNN finished applying the last of the cream-toned nursery trim paint.

Even though it'd been a while since he'd been gone, Tristan's words still resonated deep within Brynn. Though she'd refused to admit it, he was right about parenting—especially when it came to handling it all on her own. But then what made him an expert? Did he even have a child of his own? She had enough of a financial cushion to last a few weeks after her daughter's birth, but after that, she'd juggle infant care, housework and cooking with a job.

Did the thought scare her? You bet. But even more terrifying was the notion of once again giving up control.

With Cayden soon to be home, Brynn popped the lid on the paint can and washed her brush in the bathroom sink.

Her baby had been extra active and the kicks and rolls had taken a toll on Brynn's lower back. Navigating the stairs proved tough, so she took her time, keeping a firm hold on the rail.

By the time she'd reached the bottom, Cayden's bus screeched to a stop, so she put on a brave face and smiled when opening the screen door to greet him. "Hey, sweetie! Have a fun day?"

"Yeah!" He crushed her in a drive-by hug before racing through the house to bolt out the back door. "He finished! My fort's done!"

For all the frustration she'd felt for Tristan, watching her son climb the ladder of the fort's slide filled her with an entirely different emotion—gratitude. No matter how much she wanted to believe she could handle every aspect of her life on her own, in this particular mission, he'd proved her wrong. And considering how resolute she felt in her belief to hold tight to her independence, she hated that chink in her shiny new defensive armor.

"Mom!" Cayden hollered from his swinging bridge. "Come play pirate with me! We can use sticks for swords!"

Heart melting with love for her sweet son, Brynn not

only made it across the yard to grab "sabers" from the brush pile, but she managed to hold her own against the cutest pirate she knew. Her happiness in the moment would've been complete, save for the lingering reminder that the only reason her son's smile shone so bright was because of Tristan's generosity with his time, strength and above-average assembly skills.

"Yoo hoo!"

The next morning, Brynn was too pregnant to attempt ducking behind a bush to avoid her elderly neighbor, Georgia Booth. Having successfully dodged her for months, the effort itself had grown more tiring for Brynn than the fear of letting yet another new person into her life.

Kneeling in her front flower bed, planting marigolds she'd found on sale at D-Shawn's, Brynn gave her neighbor a wave. "Good morning, Mrs. Booth!"

In ten seconds flat, the white-haired woman made it across the street and into Brynn's yard. "Fine day for planting."

"That it is." Rocking back on her heels, Brynn smiled. "Your elephant ear bed makes me crazy with envy."

Georgia reddened and the size of her grin tugged at Brynn's heart. "Nice of you to notice. I planted those bulbs when my Harold—bless his soul—was off fighting in the South Pacific. They were so exotic. Made me feel closer to him."

"What a nice story. Knowing the history of how those gorgeous plants came to be makes me love them even more." Not to mention, wish she had more happy memories of her own. Mack's death and resulting scandals had soiled everything they'd shared to the point Brynn often felt, aside from Cayden and the baby girl about to be born, she'd have been better off never knowing Mack at all. "Your husband did come home? From the war?"

"Oh, yes. Harold finished pharmacy school and ran the corner drugstore for nearly forty years. His oddball habits drove me crazy, but I still miss him." Eyes welling, Georgia pressed her hands to her heart.

Which made Brynn teary, too. "I—I'm so sorry I haven't taken the time to get to know you sooner. Working on the house and caring for my son—well, not that any of that is a good excuse, but I've been busy."

Georgia waved off the apology. "Aren't we all? But now that we are acquainted, no more avoiding me behind your rosebushes."

Brynn gasped. All this time, Georgia had known?

"I might be old," she said with a sly grin, "but I'm not blind. Whether you like it or not, the rumor mill in this town has been churning up a storm about you. I know your whole story and it breaks my heart. Mack might've had his wild streaks, but at heart, he was a good boy. Losing him didn't just hurt you, but all of us."

Chest aching, Brynn managed, "I—I'm not sure what to say."

"No words necessary." After taking the spade from Brynn's hands, Georgia helped herself to the flat of marigolds, planting one before Brynn could even open her mouth. "Unless, of course, you want to invite me to this big birthday party I've heard your sweet Cayden is having."

"What're you wearing?"

Late Saturday morning, Tristan looked up from the spy novel he'd been trying to lose himself in to check if his mom had developed spots or a fever. Nope, just a still-flushed complexion from her latest stint on the treadmill. "Why would you ask that?"

"You are planning on going to Brynn's son's party, aren't you? You built the afternoon's main attraction—other than the birthday boy himself."

Tristan reread his latest page.

"Ignore me all you want, but not only do I think you should go, but you should wear something nice. I heard through the garden club grapevine that there will be no less than six eligible women in attendance."

He whistled. "You want me to start something with all of them or just a few?"

"Don't be fresh." She took her two-pound hand weights from the coffee table. "Wouldn't kill you to get out of here—did my heart good, seeing you help Brynn and her boy."

Weary of his mom's meddling, he marked his page and tossed his book to the sofa. "I'm mowing the lawn."

"Hasn't it only been a few days since you last did it?"

"Yeah, but it's the only place I can go without you yapping at me." He kissed her cheek. "I appreciate you caring—really, I do. But I'm good. Getting better every day."

"Then prove it by for once, shaving, then putting on a pair of khakis and a nice shirt. Since I already bought a gift for Cayden, you can just add your name to my box. Not that I was invited, but I thought you might be."

Laughing, he said, "You've covered all your bases…"

"Which reminds me—rumor has it you also volunteered to help little Cayden with his hitting. Want to tell me about that?"

Tristan winced. "Nope."

His cell rang. Andrea. Was Jack okay?

"Who is it?" his mom asked.

Already on the way to the screened back porch, he told her before answering, hating the pain in his stomach that always accompanied just hearing his ex's voice.

"Hey," he answered, arms crossed, leaning against a wood column. "Everything all right with Jack?"

"Great." Though the reception was crap, her tone struck him as breezy. As if she hadn't a care in the world. Why did she get to be happy, yet he'd basically lost everything? "Only we're on a day cruise, and I guess being on the water reminded Jack of his dad. He wants to talk to you."

"Cool." Tristan's heart soared. His biggest fear wasn't dying in a third-world country, but having his own son forget him. The fact that Jack remembered the times he and Tristan had spent on the water meant a lot.

"Dad?"

Tristan's eyes welled and he wasn't sure he could speak past the knot in his throat. "Hey, buddy! Hear you're spending a day in my favorite place."

"We're on the Pacific and this boat is pretty big, but not even kinda the size of the ships you took me on. It doesn't have awesome guns, either."

Tristan laughed through silent tears. "Did you at least bring your own weapon in case pirates attack?"

"I have my best squirt pistol, but Mom said I couldn't wear my battle helmet because I might not see good enough and fall off the boat."

"That makes sense." Wiping his cheeks with his wrist, Tristan laughed and nodded, picturing his son on the bow, fending off imaginary invaders.

"Well, I gotta go. Peter bought me food to feed the seagulls."

"Be careful," Tristan said, resenting the hell out of Andrea's new husband for assuming his role. Although with Tristan having been gone three-quarters of the last year they'd been married, how much of an active part in Jack's life had he really played? "They've got sharp beaks."

Jack laughed. "I will, Dad! Love you!"

"Love you, too, bud." Though his son had broken the connection, Tristan held his cell like a life raft, with the backs of his hands he took another swipe at his eyes.

"You okay?" His mom stepped up behind him, placing her comforting hand between his shoulder blades.

Though he was anything but *okay,* for her sake, he nodded. "I'm good. Sounds like he's gonna have a great day."

"How about you?"

"What do you mean?" Still unable to face anyone, he stared out at the lush backyard, focusing on the sweet-smelling honeysuckle winding up his mom's pagoda. The quick-growing plant already needed a trim.

"I mean, are you going to Cayden's party? Or you gonna sit around here and mope?"

"Mom," he managed, aching to his core. "I know you have the best intentions, but please stay out of this."

"But—"

Busting open the screen door with the heel of his hand, he strode across the backyard, intent on taking a run. Didn't matter that he only wore leather flip-flops. What mattered was running as fast and far as possible from his problems—which now happened to include his well-meaning, yet nonetheless interfering, mom.

SINCE CAYDEN'S DAD HAD BEEN gone, and he didn't make the baseball team, Cayden hadn't been sure he'd ever be happy again. But then Mr. Tristan built his pirate ship fort and now all his friends were over and brought presents and his mom made a cake and his face hurt from smiling. And there were a *really* whole lot of presents!

"Having fun?" his mom asked when he was looking at the gift table.

"Uh-huh! When can I open stuff?"

She laughed, which made him even happier. "Pretty soon. First, we all need to sing to you and let you blow out the candles on your cake."

"Okay. Is Mr. Tristan here? I want him to play pirate!"

"I haven't seen him." She looked around. "But maybe he'll be here soon?"

"Hope so! He's cool!"

Cayden went back to his fort, where his friend Dominic hung upside down while eating grape Laffy Taffy. "Well? Is Coach Tristan coming?"

"Maybe." Cayden not only told all his friends the cool SEAL would be there, but Dominic said his mom told him that Tristan was gonna help Cayden with his hitting. Cayden hoped since it was his birthday, Tristan was just waiting to tell him about it at the party.

The longer the party was, the more Cayden worried Tristan wasn't gonna come. Everyone he knew on the whole planet was there—except for his dad and old friends back in St. Louis. Even Coach Jason and his wife and their bad little kid were in the backyard.

For a few minutes, while blowing out his candles and opening presents, Cayden forgot about his new grown-up friend, but it was weird, no matter how many great toys he got, he still felt kinda sad about not seeing Tristan.

"You were kind to invite an old geezer like me to your son's big day." Georgia helped herself to seconds of Cayden's chocolate, pirate-themed cake.

"Stop," Brynn said from the lawn chair she was embarrassingly trapped in. "You get around far better than I do. Pretty sure I'm stuck."

In a flash, Georgia was up and had Brynn's hands, tugging her to her feet.

"Thanks." Laughing, Brynn was surprised by the easy camaraderie she felt with the neighbor she'd avoided for so long. Yet in the same respect, the snippets of happiness she stole like this were what stood to hurt the most should her world once again fall apart.

Georgia had already returned her focus to cake. "Kindly don't sit again until I'm done."

"I won't," Brynn promised.

"Is that Tristan?"

Was it wrong that just hearing his name caused Brynn's heart to skip a beat? Striving for a casual tone, she asked, "Where?"

"He's gone now, but I swear I just saw him pulling one of your old tricks and ducking behind my hedge." With a put-out sigh, she dropped her paper cake plate back to the picnic table. "At this rate, I'll never satisfy my sweet tooth."

Though the party was in full swing around her, classic Beach Boys playing on the ancient stereo she'd hauled outside, and practically every soul she'd met since moving to Ruin Bayou milling about her backyard, Brynn's gaze—her very breath—felt centered around the sight of Georgia tugging a sheepish-looking Tristan from behind her overgrown forsythia.

Chapter Five

"Ouch." Nothing served as more of a reminder that Tristan had lost his SEAL's edge than being yanked by his ear out from under defensive cover by a woman old enough to be his great-grandmother.

"Don't you 'ouch' me, young man. I'm still miffed at you from when you stole bubble gum from our drugstore."

"Mrs. Booth, I was eight, and not only did I return it, but I wrote you a formal apology."

She snorted. "Kids today, think you can get away with anything. Now, why are you snooping on Brynn's party? Weren't you invited?"

"Sure, I was invited, I just—"

"Don't want to get too close to Cayden because he reminds you of Jack?"

Having been raised on the ideal that if he didn't have anything nice to say then he shouldn't say anything at all, Tristan clamped his mouth tight. Damn this busybody town. Why hadn't he taken leave in Miami or Vegas?

"Go ahead and be mad at me." Georgia was back to tugging, only this time she'd grabbed hold of his arm and was pulling him toward the party. "But when you get to my age, I don't much care who thinks what and I call things like I see 'em. Ask me, you and Brynn and Cayden would make a nice family. She's gonna need a man around, what with her new baby on the way."

On that nutty note, Tristan had lost all patience. "Not only am I not in the market for a new wife, I'm still not over my old one." Their official split may have been three years ago, but for him, it hadn't seemed real until Andrea's unexpected wedding and sudden move. "Pretty sure Brynn feels the same."

"Snippy, huh?" Instead of looking properly chastised, Georgia grinned. "Only proves my point."

Thankfully, Brynn's mouthy neighbor returned to her chair and cake.

Though he knew everyone in Brynn's yard, Tristan felt like an outsider. He had nothing in common with these people anymore. When he'd come home with Andrea and Jack in tow, his life had been in sync with his friends'. He and Jason talked fishing or sports while their wives dissed them on everything from leaving clothes on the floor to drinking milk from the carton. Jason's wife, Trina, had been pregnant with their son Nathan during Tristan and Andrea's last trip to town. Trina had been so happy in her pregnancy, she glowed. It'd brought back good memories of Andrea carrying Jack.

Eyeing very pregnant Brynn, Tristan wasn't sure what to think. It went without saying, she was off-the-charts adorable—not that her looks mattered.

When she glanced up, almost as if having felt his stare, he died even more than when Georgia had caught him behind her bushes. "Hi," she said, sounding so much from the north.

Everyone he knew from down south said *hey*. Not that it mattered. Just a thought to further put off the embarrassment of talking to her now that he'd been busted spying on her son's big day.

"Cayden hoped you'd come." She ducked her gaze.

"Me, too. Can I get you some cake?"

Mouth dry, he nodded. "Sounds good. And sorry about that." He gestured toward Georgia's yard. "Truth be told, I wasn't sure if I wanted to come. Nothing personal, you understand, just…" He stopped short of admitting how painful it was, being in the presence of boys nearly the same age as his son.

"I get it." When she curved her slight fingers to his forearm, the warmth and comfort stemming from her simple touch felt akin to sipping his mother's honeyed tea when battling a cold. Casting a shy smile, she shocked him by admitting, "I've done the same."

While he tried and failed in coming up with a witty reply, she cut him a generous corner piece of her son's cake. In passing the plate, their hands brushed. He wanted to ignore the faint rush of awareness—as if he were back in junior high and passing notes with the hottie sitting in front of him in English—but despite his best efforts, even after the fleeting moment passed, the sensation had not.

"Good to see you, man." Jason delivered a light smack to his shoulder. After general small talk about high school kids having spray painted their school mascot on Polk Bayou bridge, and Trina pulling Brynn aside to discuss her potato salad recipe, Jason asked, "Vivian told me you want to privately coach Cayden. That true?"

"I s'pose." Tristan tossed his plate and fork in a nearby trash can. He knew now he should never have made the offer. Being around Cayden might be good for the boy, but it would bring nothing but added pain for himself. "Though since his mom seems against it, I'll probably steer clear of the whole situation."

"Not so fast." Jason downed the rest of his punch. "Your offer got me to thinking. Little Cayden was pretty torn up about not making the team, and Oliver Crouch's mom called last night to tell me they're probably moving. Since you already agreed to be my assistant coach, what do you think of going ahead and letting Cayden join his friends? Assuming you'll get him up to speed."

Tristan tipped his gaze to the sun, covering his face with his hands. The day he'd made that offer, Vivian had been a full-on bitch to Brynn. It hadn't been right, and his suggestion to help had shut her up. He couldn't have said then why he'd done it, meaning he sure as hell didn't know now. All he did know was that he felt backed into a corner on the whole issue and didn't like it. On his own with Brynn, when they'd stood side by side at her clothesline, and warm sun beat down on them and the smell of those fresh-washed clothes brought on sentimental longings for his more simple, younger years, he'd made that speech to her about everything being easier with a team. But after the painful call with his son, for his own self-preservation, he needed to retreat. "For the record, I never said I'd be your assistant coach."

His old friend grinned. "Pretty sure you did."

Tristan sighed. "Look, I need to start thinking about getting back to the base. I'm out of shape and—"

Jason whistled loud enough to get everyone's attention. "Someone mind temporarily killing the music?"

One of the older kids obliged.

"Seeing as this is Cayden's birthday, my friend Tristan and I have cooked up a little surprise."

"Jason…" Tristan said under his breath. "I never agreed to squat."

"What is it, Coach? Hi, Tristan!" Cayden stood in front of them.

For Tristan, the kid's huge grin and jumping brought on a wicked case of indigestion.

"Not sure if you knew this," Jason said to the boy, "but your dad and I were good friends. He was the greatest ball player to ever come out of this town—heck, the whole state. Because of that, I'm betting somewhere inside you is just as great a hitter. You only need a little extra practice to coax him out."

Cayden cocked his head. "What's that mean?"

His mom stood behind him, her hands on his slight shoulders. "Jason…"

"All that means," the coach said, "is that Tristan is going to teach you a few things about the game, and I'm inviting you to play with the Mud Bugs."

"But I wasn't good enough to make the team."

Ruffling his hair, Jason said, "When we had tryouts, I could tell you were having an off day. With Tristan's help, in a couple weeks, you'll be hitting with the best of us. Right, guys?"

Team members and friends had gathered around the birthday boy. Taking Jason's lead, they all encouraged him and welcomed him to the team.

Only for Tristan to hear, Brynn said, "As much as I appreciate what you and Jason are doing, my son doesn't need charity. What if after all this hoopla, he still isn't good enough to keep up with the rest of the team? How's his heart going to bear once again losing, when he's already lost so much?"

"Can't tell you," Tristan admitted, shoving his hands in his pockets. He didn't like Brynn's assumption that she or her son would come out losers in any situation. Which was no doubt why he surprised even himself by admitting, "But if this were my son? I'd at least want to take the chance. What if Cayden does improve? What if he not only gets to spend the summer hanging out with his friends, but feels more connected with his dad through their shared love of the game?"

Turning introspective, she averted her gaze. "I didn't know you had a son. And I hadn't thought of it like that."

Neither had he. But it was true.

As much as Tristan hated the thought of another man raising his son, he also knew in his heart Peter was doing right by Jack. Andrea and Tristan would always have their issues, but in large part due to Peter, their negativity had had little impact on their son.

What would Mack think about Tristan helping Cayden?

Back in school, Mack, Jason and Tristan had been tight. After high school, they'd gone their separate ways—no one more so than the pro ballplayer, but they'd all been raised on the core belief that your friends were friends for life. If Mack or Jason had needed him, Tristan would always be there. So why, when Mack had been in way over his head, hadn't he reached for friends' helping hands?

Tristan found himself needing to ask, "Did Mack ever show signs of being in trouble?"

She shook her head. "The day of his shooting, we were at the kitchen bar, deciding when to tell Cayden he'd be getting a baby brother or sister. Our life together was so blessed—like living in a wonderful dream—that when he was gone, part of me had a hard time even comprehending Mack died."

Music once again played, and without much else going on for a warm Saturday twilight, while their children darted amongst Spanish moss and lightning bugs, adults shared stories and laughs around dancing citronella candles.

"This party," she continued, "is the most connected I've felt to our old life in a while. This is how things used to be. We were always surrounded by friends. But once the scandal broke, so did those bonds. Cayden and I were treated like pariahs for things we hadn't even known about, let alone participated in. That's why I've been so hesitant about making new friends here. Who's to say they won't all leave, as well?"

Tristan felt compelled to lighten the mood. "Well, first, as you could probably tell, us Louisianans love nothing more than eating—especially when the food's free."

She cracked a smile. "I have noticed every event down here is accompanied by a meal."

He nodded. "And second, we have a way of attaching and sticking around—kind of like a tick, only with far better manners and no chance of fever."

Laughing, she said, "Not sure if that makes me feel much better, but thanks for trying."

"Anytime." Her laugh was contagious and suddenly all he wanted to do was shake off the gloom that'd settled over him ever since Andrea and Jack's move. For the first time in he couldn't remember when, he was tired of moping and wanted to enjoy the beautiful night with an equally beautiful woman.

TUCKING THE SARAN WRAP INTO the drawer beside the stove, Brynn said, "This day—and night—turned out different than I'd planned."

"It was a really great party. Dom fell asleep before I could get his shoes off."

Well past midnight, Cayden and Dominic had crashed

on the living-room sleeper sofa. Vivian and Sean helped put any food that might spoil in the fridge. The rest, Brynn told them she'd tackle in the morning.

"Thanks again for your help." Brynn crushed her friend in a hug. Vivian had her catty moments, but all the work she'd done helping Brynn with Cayden's special day more than made up for her most recent nasty remarks.

"My pleasure." Vivian politely covered her yawn, then took her purse from the counter. "You know who else seemed to have an especially good time once the zydeco started playing?"

"Who?" Sean asked. Up to this point, he'd done as little work as possible, doing his part by finishing off the remains of mostly eaten bowls and platters. Now he'd moved on to bags of chips.

"Not that I was talking to you," Vivian said, "but since you're nosing into our business, I mean Tristan."

"I'm sitting right here." Sean waved his latest bag of Doritos. "How is it not my business?"

Back to her usual self, Vivian rolled her eyes. "Because I'm talking to Brynn. Last thing I want is for you and your gossipy friends to start discussing our business. When you overheard me and—"

"Okay, whoa…" Brynn held up her hands. "Last thing I want is to get in the middle of a family squabble."

"You're not," Vivian assured. "I just thought it notable that Tristan not only danced with you, but honest-to-goodness laughed. You two have something going on I don't know about?"

"Of course not." Brynn grabbed the dishrag and gave the counter a good wipe. "We're barely even friends."

"But he built Cayden's fort?"

Brynn nodded.

"He also mowed your lawn. And let's not forget that daring swamp rescue."

"Gotta admit," Sean said between bites, "that had to be pretty exciting, Brynn. You and Cayden getting saved by a SEAL? I was a couple years behind Tristan and his crew in high school, but they seemed like good guys."

Brynn put away air-dried pots and pans. "For the record, Jason found Cayden. And anyway, I'm sure we'd have eventually stumbled our way out."

Sean shook his head. "Been a lot of folks vanish in that swamp over the years."

"Oh, stop." Vivian swatted him with a towel. "All I'm saying is it's fairly obvious you two share chemistry. What would it hurt for you to, say…explore?"

"What would it hurt?" Brynn pointed at her bulging belly and laughed. What she didn't do was confess she'd not only felt that chemistry, but used every trick in her womanly arsenal to fight it.

SUNDAY AFTERNOON, TRISTAN struggled with his decision to help Cayden with his hitting not so much because the kid reminded him of Jack, but because of a whole new batch of troubles revolving around Cayden's mom.

While the boy gathered the dozen brightly painted balls that'd scattered over the field, Tristan couldn't stop himself from stealing a quick glance into the stands. Pretty as you please, there sat Brynn, holding an umbrella to shade her from the sun in one hand and a fan in her other. She'd crammed her mess of red curls into a ponytail and strays popped out at all angles. Hell, she looked like a ginger-toned, half-blown dandelion. For the life of him, he couldn't imagine her in the role of a pro-ballplayer's polished wife. But then by her own admission, things for her and Cayden had changed an awful lot since then.

"Mom!" Cayden shouted after tossing a ball farther than he ever had. "Did you see that?"

"Yes, sir, I did! You're getting better already!"

Glowing from his mother's praise, Cayden's grin stretched ear to ear. Which, in turn, made Brynn smile. Lord, she was pretty when she smiled. Saturday night, once Cayden's party had morphed into more of a grown-up affair, she'd closed her eyes, smiling while swaying to zydeco. Sweat flushed her freckled cheeks and chest and damn if Tristan could recall having ever seen a sexier pregnant woman.

"Got 'em all, Coach Tristan!"

Brynn's son's voice jolted Tristan to the present. With the balls back at his feet, he said, "Great. Now we're gonna do it all over again. Remember, you can't even swing at the ball unless it's the color I call out."

"But that's too hard. Why can't we just hit the regular way?"

"Because this is going to help your mind slow down enough to really see the ball. Right now, we just want you to hit most anything an opposing team's pitcher throws. But eventually, you're going to have to recognize fastballs and curveballs and all kinds of other pitches you haven't yet seen."

"Oh." A steeled mask of determination Tristan swore he'd once seen on Mack's face settled over the boy's features. Maybe he had some of his dad's playing skill in him after all?

In the stands, Brynn had leaned forward as far as her baby bump allowed. She'd abandoned her umbrella and fan to cross her fingers. Her hopeful expression was all the motivation Tristan needed to continue working with her son for as long as it took to make the game sink in. Only Tristan's goal wasn't so much about Cayden one day playing in the majors, but selfishly making Brynn smile again.

"WELL, HELLO. YOU MUST be Cayden's mother, Brynn."

From her seat in the empty stands, Brynn looked up to see a middle-aged woman with short salt-and-pepper hair and Tristan's grin carrying an insulated jug and red Solo cups.

"I'm Donna. Tristan's mom. I figured the boys would be thirsty out in this sun." She wagged the jug and ice shifted inside.

"I know I am," Brynn said with a laugh. "Nice to meet you and great idea."

Donna waved off the compliment. "When you've been a Little League mom for as many years as I have, you learn a few tricks along the way."

Out on the field, Tristan called to Cayden, "What's going on with your grip? Remember how we talked about lining up your knuckles for a box grip?"

Biting his lower lip, Cayden nodded and realigned his hands.

"Good," Tristan said. "Holding the bat with your palms can give you a pretty nasty bruise—no fun."

"He's awfully good with kids," Brynn said to Donna. "Earlier, when the whole team was here, he never lost his patience."

"He probably learned from his father." Donna poured Brynn a lemonade. "When Tristan's dad died—my Jim—it took a lot out of him. Tristan's son, Jack, was a newborn at the time and Tristan poured all his grief into living for his son. Every time he shipped out on a mission, I know Tristan worried himself sick over keeping himself safe. Last thing he wanted was to leave his boy. So when his ex carted Jack off to California..." Donna's expression darkened. "Let's just say it's been hard on us both."

"If you don't mind my asking, what happened? Tristan's not exactly chatty about his past."

"No..." After wiping sudden tears, his mother said, "Three years ago, he came home from six months in Afghanistan to find his house empty. Andrea and Jack gone. It was like a movie scene. So cruel. She hadn't moved far, though, so I think in Tristan's mind, as long as he got to see Jack as often as he liked, nothing much had changed. But then about a month ago, the man Andrea had been seeing accepted a job in L.A. He proposed and fast as a twister, swept Jack from Tristan's life. The shock of it led to him making near-critical mistakes on his last mission. His commander sent him home— said in his current frame of mind he was unfit for duty. Tristan was devastated. Scares me to death when I think how much worse this all could've turned out if he'd been hurt—or any of his friends." She took a deep, shuddering breath, then forced a smile. "Anyway...helping your Cayden is good for my son, and I appreciate you letting Tristan into your boy's life."

"I'm the one who's thankful." Brynn's throat tightened upon seeing Tristan's mother again grow teary. To mask her own feelings after hearing Tristan's heartbreaking story, Brynn sipped the refreshingly sweet drink. Poor guy. No wonder he hadn't felt like talking about what he'd been through. She wished there was something she could do to ease his pain, but as she'd learned all too well, when it came to a failed marriage, there wasn't much anyone could do. "Learning this game means the world to Cayden."

Donna beamed. "Then it looks like both of our sons stand to win."

When Tristan caught sight of his mom, he waved, which was all the signal Donna needed to head out onto the field.

Brynn initially thought to follow, but held back.

Saturday night, after sleepy kids had been put to bed, Cayden's party had taken a new turn. Sean and a few of the other team dads had made a quick run to the store. The birthday transformed into a barbecue with plenty of beer, steaks, blackened chicken and a huge pot simmering with potatoes, crawfish, spices and corn on the cob.

Though Brynn obviously hadn't imbibed, plenty of others had—not to the point of drunkenness, but just enough to loosen the mood. After dinner, dancing followed and whew, Tristan knew a few sexy moves. Though he never even touched her, he'd somehow generated a staggering amount of physical heat—not a good thing considering her condition and her vow to never again need a man.

She looked up from the stands to catch him staring.

His grin launched fireworks in her midsection.

Okay, so while she would never *need* a man, what were the rules about *wanting* one?

Chapter Six

"How was Cayden's first lesson with Tristan?"

"Good." Monday afternoon, Brynn sat with Vivian in Bremwall's Sporting Goods, waiting for the boys to be fitted for their Mud Bug uniforms. Thankfully, Assistant Coach Tristan was not in attendance.

"Just good?"

Brynn shifted on the too-small chair. "I wasn't expecting that after one visit with Tristan, Cayden would be called to the majors."

"I wasn't talking about your son's hitting, but how you feel with his coach. After seeing you two dance Saturday night, I didn't want to let on too much in front of Sean, but I swear I detected sparks."

Sighing, Brynn tried for a count of ten to regain patience with Vivian, but she only made it to three. "For the last time, Tristan and I are friends—nothing more. He's a great guy for helping my son. End of story."

Vivian rolled her eyes.

Once Cayden was finally measured and Brynn had written a hefty check, covering everything from custom T-shirts, socks, shoes, game uniform, batting helmet and three hats, she made a note to check her bank balance to see if they had enough cash left for groceries.

As soon as she had her baby girl, as much as Brynn

would hate leaving her, she had no choice but to find a job. The marketing degree she'd once been so proud to have earned seemed a bit silly in Ruin Bayou—not that she'd ever used it in St. Louis. Being Mack's wife had been a full-time position.

"You going to be at tonight's practice?" Vivian asked. She was next in line to pay. "If you are, I'll bring my baby name books for us to flip through."

"Sounds good."

Outside, Cayden said, "Can you believe how much stuff I get, Mom? Isn't this, like, the most exciting thing *ever?*"

"Sure is…" Squelching the knot of financial worry in her throat, Brynn dug through her purse for the car keys, but was unsuccessful. Figuring she must've left them on the counter when she paid, she'd just turned to go back into the store when she almost collided with Tristan.

"Whoa!" He laughed. "This place ought to put up caution signs to protect folks from charging pregnant ladies."

"Ha-ha."

He and Cayden high-fived.

"Coach Tristan, I'm gonna get brand-new *everything!* And lots of it is even gonna have my name on it, just like Dad's used to have."

"That's cool, bud. Glad you're excited. I'm here to get my uniform, too. Coach Jason said if I didn't come today, I'd be in big trouble."

"Wow…" Cayden widened his eyes. "He said that to me, too. That must mean we're important."

"Guess so." Glancing to Brynn, Tristan asked, "How are you? Got everything back in shape after Saturday night?"

"Finally." Had his shoulders always been so broad or

his teeth so white? "Returned the last of the borrowed lawn chairs to neighbors this morning."

"You shouldn't be lifting. I'd have been happy to help."

"Thanks, but it wasn't a big deal." *Dancing with you, however…*

When she caught his gaze, he held it until her breathing slowed. Until the other parents and kids leaving the store vanished and the two of them stood on their own island. Until she couldn't remember what had even brought her to the store. And then she was looking away, licking her lips, wondering, wondering what had just happened?

"Looking for these?" Vivian had somehow ended up beside her, jingling Brynn's lost keys.

"Ah, thanks." It took Brynn a moment to recover from whatever *hadn't* happened between Tristan and her. "I was just headed back inside to look for them."

"But instead," Vivian said with an exaggerated wink, "you found this big lug." Turning to Tristan, she asked, "Doesn't Brynn look pretty today? I love her upswept hair. And what do you call this style of dress?" Brynn's supposed friend tugged the vibrant yellow fabric of the oversize muumuu Brynn had bought on a Los Cabos vacation with Mack. At the time, she'd been six months pregnant with Cayden and had felt pretty with the hand-crafted yarn embroidery at the neck and short sleeves. Now, the dress was a little snug. The color too bright for a small town like Ruin Bayou. "You look like you could step right into a fiesta. In fact, if you two want to try out the new Mexican place down by the river, Dom and I would be happy to take Cayden home with us. Sound fun, guys?"

"Yeah!" With both boys high-fiving, Brynn didn't have the heart to say no. On the flip side, there was no way she'd spend an evening alone with Tristan in what she'd heard was a romantic setting.

"That sounds like a great plan," Tristan said, hedging closer to the door, "but I was due inside ten minutes ago. Brynn, maybe another time?"

"Sure." Brynn's mood sagged. Even though she genuinely hadn't wanted to go, what woman enjoyed being dumped before even being asked on a date?

As abruptly as Tristan had appeared, he was gone, leaving Brynn on her own to deal with Vivian's scowl. "What's wrong with you?"

"Me?" Hands to her chest, Brynn asked, "Who was the one trying to sell me like I was a big, pregnant piñata up for auction?"

"Mom?" Dominic fished through Vivian's purse. "Where are the keys? Me and Cayden wanna watch a movie in the car."

"Cayden—" Brynn tugged her son closer by the back of his shirt "—come on with me. You can go to Dom's another night."

"But, Mom…" he whined. *"Please."*

"Sorry for being a buttinski matchmaker," Vivian said, "but don't punish the boys for my mistake. Let Cayden come over and you take the time to relax. I'll bring him home later. You won't have to do a thing, other than put your feet up."

The offer did hold appeal. "All right, but really, Viv, promise you'll never do anything like that again and drop this romance you've spun between Tristan and me. It's not going to happen."

"Scout's honor." After holding up three fingers in an

awkward salute, Vivian pulled Brynn into a hug. "You just go on home and have a nice night. Forget any of this even happened."

EASIER SAID THAN DONE.

Especially when Brynn was jolted from a lovely cat-nap by a knock on the front door. Even worse, when she parted the curtains she found Tristan bearing flowers she was fairly certain had come from Georgia Booth's side yard.

"Hey," he said with a sleepy grin that somersaulted her already sketchy tummy. "Brought you these. My feeble attempt at apologizing for Vivian's crazy match-making."

She accepted his purple rhododendrons. "Thanks, but it wasn't your fault." Eyeing the pretty bouquet, she had to ask, "You didn't steal these from my neighbor, did you?"

"No," he said with great offense. "And hand deliver that crazy woman more reason to dislike me? Give me some credit. They're from my own mom's yard—with her blessing."

Brynn's face overheated. "You told Donna about that awkward exchange at the store?"

"Just in passing." When Brynn stood back from the door, he brushed past, flooding her with scents of sun, sweat and leather from the sporting goods store. Any normal time in her life, this would've been no big deal, but superpregnant with raging hormones to match left her in constant flux when it came to her feelings regarding the man. "Have a seat. I want to get these in water."

"Sure."

Time away from him—however brief—would be welcome. He'd already done enough to distract her. Distract her from what, she couldn't say. The mere act of being around him had her addled mind waffling in a danger zone between attraction and irritation. After all she'd been through, her body hadn't gotten the memo that romance was permanently out of her picture.

Foiling her plan for escape, he trailed after her. "Looked like Cayden was pretty psyched about getting his uniform."

"Oh, he was. But when it came time to pay the bill, I nearly had this baby on the spot."

Leaning against the counter while she filled a clear blue vase with water, he said, "Not that it's my business, but Mack didn't leave you financially okay?"

She laughed. "Um, no. Upon his death, his assets were frozen. Authorities seized the house, but let me keep his pricey car. I sold it, but after the funeral, paying creditors and legal fees to prove I hadn't been involved in any of Mack's schemes, there's hardly anything left. Soon as the baby's born, I need a job."

He winced. "Good ones aren't easy to come by around here. Partly why I went into the navy."

"If I didn't have Cayden, and his baby sister on the way, I would consider that route." She set the flowers on the center of the kitchen table. They looked pretty. "Can you believe I used to keep a florist on speed dial? Our St. Louis home had a grand foyer with a center table. Mack liked it topped with a giant vase of fresh flowers—the kind you'd see in a hotel lobby."

Tristan whistled. "Too bad you can't have a little of that cash back in your pocket."

"No kidding," Brynn said with a sad chuckle. She forced a breath and smile then changed the subject. "It's a gorgeous night. Wanna take a pregnant lady for a walk before her rowdy kid comes home?"

"I'd be honored." Always a gentleman, he offered her his arm.

She politely declined.

NOT WANTING TO GIVE CAYDEN the wrong idea about possibly becoming a regular fixture in the little boy's home, Tristan left before Vivian dropped him off.

Back at his mom's, he found a note about her being at one of her friends', playing bunko. He nuked the dinner she'd left in the fridge, then settled into his dad's old recliner to watch the Cards take on the Cubs.

The more he heard about Mack, the more disappointed he grew in his old friend. Mack had been given the world on a proverbial platter. Dream job. Amazing wife. Cute, smart kid. Where had it all gone wrong?

But then he supposed the same could be asked about Tristan's own life. Or could it? For years, he'd beaten himself up over the breakup of his marriage, but he hadn't been the one leaving. Andrea knew going into their relationship that he didn't exactly have an ordinary job. Why had she waited until they'd had a child to cry foul?

His mom came home, handing him a plate of cookies before settling in to her nightly crafts and reality shows.

When Tristan felt more focused on figuring out where he'd gone wrong with his ex than watching the game, he wandered into the room his mom called her "Lady Lair." When he'd been a kid, it'd been a guest room, but all of the visiting dowager aunts had died and he was glad Donna had found a new use for the good-size space.

"What's up?" she asked when he stood in the doorway.

"I don't know." Raking his fingers through his too long hair, he sighed. "Somehow, I ended up back at

Brynn's again and she talked about her finances. Seems like Mack left her in a pretty bad spot. Which got me to thinking where he'd gone off course."

"Good question," she murmured with a row of straight pins clamped between her lips. The project of the week was dolls for a Shreveport women's shelter. She'd formed an assembly line of dress pieces nearly ready to sew. "He was raised pretty much the same as the rest of you. Maybe the big city and all that attention went to his head?"

"I guess." Tristan sat on a dainty floral upholstered armchair that made him feel oversize and awkward. "But I guess the point I was getting to is that he had it all and threw it away. As great a gal as Brynn is, that made me mad. But on the flip side, is that what I did with Andrea? She begged me, for the sake of our family, to quit the navy and I wouldn't do it. Now I'm so torn up over her taking Jack, I'm not even fit for duty."

"First," she said over the sewing machine's hum, "any woman who marries a serviceman knows up front what she's getting into. I died a million deaths when your dad was in Vietnam, but that didn't give me permission to quit on our vows. Second, don't you dare take on the guilt for your marriage ending. Of course, it would've been nice had you been home more often, but when you enter a life of service, it's not like you get to pick and choose your hours. Third—" She shook her head and growled. "I don't even have a third. All I know is by moving a whole country away, she didn't just take your child, but my grandchild. And that stings."

"Sure does." Hurting even worse was the sudden craving to see Brynn. He hardly knew the woman. Why would he want her any further ingrained in his life?

THURSDAY NIGHT, TEN MINUTES into a crowded Mud Bug parent meeting being held in the library's community room, Brynn wished she'd accepted Vivian's offer to take notes and deliver any must-know information later.

The space was too small and stuffy, smelling of a strong blend of perfume and cologne. The longer her pregnancy dragged on, the greater her sense of smell grew and the more scents she disliked. Toss in her achy lower back and nausea and she was not a happy camper.

"This seat taken?"

"Um, no." But one glance into Tristan's dark eyes had her wishing it was. She wasn't in her right mind around him—especially not when the cramped space had the entire length of her left side crushed against him. And he smelled too good—if there could even be such a thing—as though he'd just showered and brushed his gorgeous white teeth.

"Glad you're here," he said while the team's booster club president handed out information sheets. "There's a batting cage at a sports complex over in Shreveport. I think it'd really do Cayden some good. He seems to do better when you're watching, so maybe you could come, too? Tomorrow night? I'll pick you up at five?"

"O-okay. Sure." The meeting might've started, but that did little to stop the chatter in Brynn's head. She and Tristan were just friends, so why was her heart racing as if he'd asked her on a date? He'd explained how he felt about jumping into another relationship and, Lord knew, she wasn't looking, so why couldn't her body get the memo that the man was only a friend?

The meeting wound on for an hour and at the end, Brynn found herself writing yet another check.

To Tristan, she tried lightening her mood by quipping, "Think I liked baseball a lot better back in the days when the team paid Mack to play, rather than the other way around."

"Yeah, it's crazy how much all of this costs, but the kids sure do enjoy it."

Brynn winced, clutching her lower back.

"You okay?" His tender look of concern was too much. Made it damn near impossible to stick to her rule of being a self-sufficient island—not that she'd done such a great job at it lately. "You're due pretty soon, aren't you?"

She nodded, forcing a smile through more pain. "In a couple weeks."

"Think you might be going into back labor? My ex went through it with my son. We kept watching for all the usual signs—water breaking and stuff, only none of it ever came. Finally, her pain was too much and we ran her to the E.R. Good thing—" his sharp exhale was followed by a smile "—she ended up having Jack two hours later."

"Yikes." Gathering her lightweight jacket from the back of her chair, Brynn said, "You got lucky. Otherwise, you might've been one of those couples you hear about being forced to deliver their babies on the side of the road."

Hand on the small of her back, he ushered her into the warm night. The fresh air did wonders for clearing Brynn's head. It made it possible to ignore the pleasant tingle still humming from Tristan's briefest touch. He was her friend. And Cayden's. Nothing more. They were lucky to have had him enter their lives.

As for the surprise she felt over him opening up to her about his past? She chose to ignore that, too. Far from him keeping illegal activity from her the way Mack had done, Tristan was only keeping a tight rein on his own pain.

He said, "I helped deliver a baby in Botswana."

"Really?" Her eyebrows raised.

"There were midwives and stuff," he said, turning red, "but they sent me on lots of missions—fetching fresh water and clean cloth. For lying on a mat in a dirt-floored hut, the mother brought whole new meaning to the expression 'grace under fire.'"

Brynn shuddered to think of having her baby girl anywhere other than the specialty birthing wing of the small regional hospital where she'd already made arrangements. It bothered her that she'd be alone, but it wasn't as if her aunt and uncle would be able to make the trip all the way from Maine. Even if they would, Brynn had this handled.

"Hey, Mom!" Cayden rounded the building's corner, ambushing her in a hug. "While you guys were meeting, we've been doing catching drills. I caught three balls!"

"That's awesome, baby!" She kissed the top of his head.

"I'm not a baby!" His pout returned. "That's the baby." Pointing at her stomach, he added, "And she's gonna ruin everything."

Thankfully, Cayden ran off to be with his friends, which gave Brynn a chance to regroup.

"Not to get in your business," Tristan said alongside her, "but seems like I felt the same about my sister. Once I saw how cute she was—all those tiny fingers and toes—I figured the whole baby sister thing might not be so bad. Want me to talk with him?"

"Thanks," she said with an exhausted sigh, "but somehow I have to believe everything's going to work out."

"Yoo-hoo!"

Brynn's stomach tightened. After receiving the morning freeze from her son, who'd climbed on his school bus without even a verbal goodbye, let alone a kiss or hug, the last thing she needed was a visit from her neighbor. All Brynn wanted was to be left alone with her thoughts and plants—which thankfully, never talked back!

"Hi, Mrs. Booth." Out of common courtesy, Brynn waved.

Charging across the street, Georgia was all smiles. "Great news!"

"Oh?" Brynn kept weeding her impatiens bed.

"Usually the garden club only accepts potential new members once a year, but considering your skill—and of course, a glowing recommendation from me—I've managed to get you a provisional membership. All you have to do is come with me to the next meeting and you're in."

"Wow." Rocking back on her heels, Brynn wasn't sure how to respond. "Thank you. But with the baby due in a couple weeks and after that, I'm going to start looking for a job, I'm not sure I'll have time."

Georgia waved off her concerns. "None of us have enough time, dear. All you can do is make time for the things you love. And it's plain from the sight of this impeccable yard that you truly do love gardening."

"That I do…" A wistful smile tugged Brynn's lips. There had once been a period in her life when she'd spent whole days prettying her yard. Now, between washing and hanging clothes, cleaning and cooking, she was lucky for the two hours she stole each morning to pursue her passion. "But what does the garden club do?"

"Well, of course, we officially lunch once a month.

But beyond that, we share plant clippings and extras—everyone's always dividing bulbs and such."

"So there's an opportunity to get free plants?"

"Every meeting. Want to tag along with me this afternoon?"

STILL RIDING THE HIGH from receiving not just a few plant cuttings, but literally dozens of exotic bulbs and whole flats of annuals, rather than dreading her and Cayden's outing with Tristan, Brynn looked forward to it, taking extra time with her hair and makeup.

Though Cayden sat downstairs scowling that she wasn't hurrying, she refused to let his impatience bring her down.

Once again, she felt grateful to Georgia. The garden club women couldn't have been more welcoming. Brynn had worried she wouldn't fit in, or considering her rocky past they'd have treated her poorly, but the day was perfect, right down to the key lime pie served for dessert. Another plus: Tristan's mom, Donna, was a member. In talking with her, Brynn had even learned of a few possible job leads.

In deference to the day's muggy heat, Brynn piled her red curls high, fastening them with rhinestone pins. Though they were only going to a batting cage, her limited maternity wardrobe didn't allow for a whole lot of options. Either she wore stretch-waisted shorts, jeans or a sundress. Opting for a pale blue floral dress, she added pearl earrings and more lip gloss than usual.

From downstairs came the muted ring of the house line phone.

A few minutes later, Cayden charged up the stairs. "Mom! Some guy's on the phone!"

"Hello?" Brynn answered. "Yes... But how? I don't

understand…" After ten more minutes of the man's droning voice, Brynn's knees buckled and she dropped to the floor.

Chapter Seven

Tristan parked his truck on Brynn's gravel drive, then whistled his way to the front porch. When he heard Cayden inside, crying for help, begging for his mom not to die, Tristan yanked open the screen door hard enough to pop the simple latch-hook closure, then charged up the stairs two at a time.

"Cayden? What's wrong?"

"Mom's dead!" The boy's face was streaked with tears. "I know she's dead! Just like my dad! I—I'm gonna be left all alone and all I know how t-to eat is cereal!"

Kneeling alongside Brynn, Tristan checked her vitals and found her pulse slightly elevated, but breathing normal. "Brynn?" he urgently coaxed. "Brynn, if you can hear me, I need you to let me know."

She groaned before delivering a drowsy nod. "I'm okay. Just give me a minute."

"Cayden," Tristan said, "you know how to dial 9-1-1?"

The still crying boy nodded.

"No, no." Brynn pressed her hands to Tristan's capable chest. "I'm fine. I just..." She shook her head. "I must've fainted—which is kind of bizarre, but considering the circumstances..."

Tristan asked, "What happened?"

Cayden had the phone. "You still want me to call?"

"Hold off for a minute, bud."

Cradling the phone, Cayden sat next to his mom, wrapping his arms around her waist. "I was so scared."

"I'm sorry, sweetie. But really, I'm fine. Just had a pretty surprising call." She managed to sit up, resting against the footboard of her brass bed.

"Who was it?" Tristan asked.

"Baseball commissioner, Ted Stevens. First, he apologized for not being able to contact me sooner, then he said they've officially closed Mack's case, all of their intended targets have been apprehended, charged and await trial, so they've not only worked with government authorities to release Mack's frozen assets, but are now prepared to make a public statement clearing him of all wrongdoing. The whole time, he was actually working *with* them. His death was a horrible accident." Covering her face with her hands, she said, "I'm not sure whether to laugh or cry. Maybe both?"

"Whoa…" That news left Tristan a little wobbly himself. "This changes everything. You could return to St. Louis and step back into your former life."

"I could. The commissioner is working with the Cardinals to host a special game in Mack's honor."

"Can we go?" Cayden asked.

"Of course." She hugged him extra close.

Tristan asked, "When do you think it'll be?"

"Later this summer." Exhaling, she curved her hands to her belly, for the first time in months, feeling as though her lungs were receiving an adequate amount of air.

"We should celebrate," Tristan said. "Hell, the whole town should throw a party. I knew from the start there was no way Mack could've been wrapped up in all that. He truly loved the game. And sounds like he loved and was wholly committed to you, too."

"Yeah…" In a heartbeat, just as abruptly as her life had changed the day of Mack's death, her whole life had once again been turned upside down, only this time for the better. "Cayden, hon? Would you please get me a cup of juice?"

Hopping to his feet, he asked, "Apple or orange?"

"Apple, please. Thanks, sweetie."

In a flash, he was off, giving Brynn the privacy she needed. "Is it wrong for a part of me to be angry all over again?" she asked Tristan. "Why did Mack lie about being part of something that tore our lives apart? And all of the sudden, I'm supposed to celebrate his glory. But how can I do that? If he walked through the front door, after everything he's put Cayden and me through, my first inclination would be to tell him to walk right back out."

Tristan sat on the floor in front of her. He inched his hands toward her—as if he might ease his fingers between hers. But he didn't. And that raised a knot in Brynn's throat that had her all the more confused.

"Look," he said with a sigh, "I can't begin to relate with what you must be going through. But for the record, I'm sorry."

"Here, Mom." Cayden thrust her juice in her face, in the process, spilling a little on the dress she'd not so long ago been excited to wear.

"Thank you, baby."

He nodded. "I'm real glad you're alive, Mom."

"Me, too." She finished her juice, then pulled him against her.

"So does your call mean Dad's alive, too? Since he's gonna be in a game?"

"Oh, baby…" His hopeful question made her especially teary on what was supposed to be a fun night for all of them. With Cayden on her lap, she stroked his hair from his forehead. "More than anything, I wish Dad was playing that game for you, but remember what we talked about? How Dad's gone forever?"

He nodded. "But I want him."

"I know, baby. I know."

WITH CAYDEN'S BATTING PRACTICE over, Tristan sat with Brynn, watching her son ride bumper cars. The miniarcade/sports complex featured enough quarter-fed activities to keep Cayden smiling for as long as it took to get the smile back on his mom's pretty face.

"Sorry about the pizza." He took her long-abandoned plate, setting it on top of his to toss in the trash. "What this place lacks in cuisine, it makes up for in fun. Wanna play minigolf?"

Her faint grin came nowhere near meeting her eyes. "You're a dear to try cheering me, but I'm afraid between my surprise call and aching back I'm not the best company."

"You're fine." He finished off his cola. "I am worried about that backache, though. Wasn't it nagging you last night, too?"

"Think it pretty much comes with the territory."

"Just to be on the safe side, how about checking it out with your doctor?"

"Sure, *Dad,*" she teased, in what he assumed was her way of trying to lighten the mood. He appreciated her effort, but didn't want her thinking she had to perform for him like a trick pony. They weren't on a date and neither was trying to impress the other. Along with being friends came a certain freedom he found comforting.

"Ha-ha." He made a funny face. "But, really, you hardly ate a thing. Want me to stop off on the way home and pick up anything else? Burger? Chicken sandwich—"

"Uh-oh…" In under thirty seconds, her expression morphed from wide-eyed surprise to wrinkled-nose displeasure to thin-lipped fear.

"What's wrong?" He looked to Cayden, but the boy was still going full force on his bumper car.

"Look." Her gaze dropped. Not only was she suddenly sitting in a puddle, but liquid had spilled off the edges of the bench seat to pool onto the red vinyl floor.

"Is that what I think it is?"

She nodded. "Pretty sure my water just broke."

"But we've got plenty of time, right?" How many combat situations had he been in? Yet during none of them had his pulse surged quite so fast.

"This is mortifying. With Cayden, I was at home when this happened. Mack was on the road, but at least I had our housekeeper to help. I'm soaked. And I can't leave this mess for—"

"Woman," he said with a growl, "you worry about the damnedest things. Right now, let's get you to a hospital."

"But I'm wet."

Think, Tristan. Think.

At the sports shop main entrance was a souvenir store featuring everything from T-shirts to purple faux Mohawk hats. Surely, they'd have something in there that was dry enough and large enough for Brynn to wear?

"Sit tight," he said to her. "I'll be right back."

He purchased oversize sweatpants and a Batting World T-shirt, then handed the manager a few twenties to not only keep an eye on Cayden, but have Brynn's water mopped up before she left the restroom.

Back with the mom-to-be, he took gentle hold of her elbow, helping her from the bench. "Stick with SEALs and your every problem will vanish."

"Oh, yeah?" Her watery-eyed smile tugged his heart-strings. He never wanted to see any woman cry, but something about Brynn's tears in particular threatened to crumple his usual steely calm.

"Come on." He steered her toward the nearest rest-room. "Let's get you cleaned up and dry. Then we'll worry about what comes next."

"But Cayden…" She looked over her shoulder. "And the mess?"

"Handled and handled. For at least the next few min-utes, all you need to worry about is you." He held open the women's room door, offering the bag with her fresh clothes. "The store had everything but…unmention-ables, so you'll have to go commando."

She winced. "That's one way of putting it."

"Need help?"

"I think I'm good." Apprehension showed in her quickened breaths and occasional winces from pain. "But if you wouldn't mind, please hang out by the door—just in case."

"You got it." Though Brynn could've only been in the restroom for a minute, time had a funny way of stretch-ing when you didn't have a clue what the next seconds might bring. Odds were, they had plenty of time to get her to the regional hospital where she'd planned for her delivery. But what if she couldn't hold out? Was the ultimate safety call getting her to a Shreveport E.R.? Lord knew, he'd been trained for every contingency from fending off nuclear armageddon to hostage rescue against impossible odds, but the one thing he had no practical knowledge of was delivering babies. That time in Botswana he'd only been an errand boy.

He knocked on the door. "Everything all right?"

"I—I think so."

"What's that mean?" His pulse surged anew. Was she having her daughter right there in the ladies' room at Batting World?

"I-if you don't mind, could you p-please come in?"

Unsure what he would see, he held his hand over his eyes. "You decent?"

"Think so..." He found her with her legs tangled in the sweatpants. She'd gotten them twisted and clung to the counter for balance. Already wearing her new T-shirt, he was glad he'd selected extra-large as it not only covered her bulging belly, but hung nearly to her knees.

"All right." Kneeling alongside her, he gently lifted one foot, then her other, straightening the soft fabric, tugging it up her even softer legs. He pulled the pants thigh high, then eased back. "Think you can take it from there?"

She nodded. "But would it be all right if I held on to you for support?"

"Of course." He laughed. "Use me any way you need."

Left hand clamped to the top of his head, she wobbled and shimmied until tugging the pants into place. Helping her in the most basic of ways did a strange thing to him—it made him want to help even more. Silly, considering he hardly knew her, but he supposed he'd feel honor-bound to help any woman in Brynn's vulnerable position.

Brynn clutched her belly. "Th-the pain, i-it's worse. Not just in my back anymore."

"Just throwing this out there—you know, in case you're open for suggestions, but maybe we should quit talking and either call you an ambulance or hightail it back to Ruin Bayou. What do you think?"

Lips clamped tight, complexion sweat-sheened, she ground out, "You're probably right. B-but I lost my purse. And my son. Do you know where Cayden is?"

"Having a great time. Oblivious to what's going down in here."

She doubled over. Her whimper ripped at his soul.

Arm around her waist, her denim floral purse slung over his left shoulder, he guided her to the dining room.

Cayden sat at a nearby table, feasting on ice cream and more pizza. "This is like the best, most funnest place *ever.*"

"Glad you liked it," Tristan said, "but we've gotta go."

"Why?" The kid's tone featured an extra serving of whine. "I've still got tokens."

"S-sweetie…" Brynn had turned deathly pale. "I—I think your sister's on the way."

"I hate her! She's not even here yet and is already ruining everything!"

As seemed usual for the boy whenever things didn't go his way, Cayden took off running.

"I—I have to go after him," Brynn said between frighteningly thin breaths.

"Correction—you *have* to either get in my truck or let me call an ambulance. Your choice."

"Truck." Clutching her lower back, she was already waddling that way. "Oh—but the mess I made in the dining room. Shouldn't we—"

"Already handled," he assured. "Just keep walking."

After settling her in the front seat of his king cab truck, Tristan tracked down Cayden to where he'd helped himself to another bumper car ride. "Get off that thing."

"You're not the boss of me!" Cayden rode farther away from Tristan.

"You're right." Tristan cut him off. "But I do care a lot about you and your mom and she's having your baby sister, so let's go."

"You're just making that up!"

Beyond frustrated, Tristan handled the situation the way he would've had Cayden been his son. He hefted the kid from the car, carrying him like a kicking and screaming sack of potatoes all the way to the truck.

"I hate you!" Cayden wailed. "Stranger danger!"

"All right," Tristan said from between clenched teeth, setting the squirmy kid to his feet, but keeping a firm hold on his forearms. "Now you've gone too far. As long as we've known each other, have I ever once hurt you?"

Cayden's chin touched his yellow T-shirt. "No. But I wanna play. And I hate that baby."

"Yeah, well, like it or not—no matter what crazy stunt you try pulling next—your sister will be here soon. And the longer you dork around, the more danger your mom is going to be in. She needs to be at a hospital. Now."

"I never thought of it like that." Cayden's voice had lost his earlier bravado. "So having my sister is bad for her?"

"If your mom doesn't have a doctor or nurse with her, it could be. I know I don't know anything about having babies, do you?"

Expression grim, Cayden shook his head.

"All right then…" Tristan released his hold on the

boy, only to offer Cayden his hand. "How about we work together to keep your mom and baby sister safe?"

With Cayden's small hand clasped in his, a dozen thoughts raced through Tristan's head. Not the least of which was how good it felt once again being a father— even if the child wasn't his own.

SOMETHING WAS WRONG.

Waiting in the truck for Cayden and Tristan, Brynn knew the pain shooting through her was too intense for early stage labor. Could her constant backaches have been labor pains and she'd been too wrapped up in baseball and the garden club to notice?

Stupid. Had she stuck to her plan of keeping to herself, her mind may have been wholly focused on her health, rather than trying to meet friends who would no doubt leave her. As for that call from the commissioner? That'd been stupid, too. The kinds of things she'd been through, what'd been done to Mack's formerly sterling reputation, they couldn't be taken back.

Biting her lower lip to keep from crying out, she instead tried shifting to a more comfortable position, gripping the dash for all she was worth.

After riding out the next wave of contractions, she was relieved to see her son running toward her. Cayden held Tristan's hand and the sweetness brought on emotional tears.

"How are you?" Tristan asked, hefting Cayden into the back, then fastening the boy's seat belt.

"I—I'm good," she lied. "But if you think you can find an E.R., I'd appreciate it. I—I'm pretty sure this baby isn't waiting to make it back to Ruin Bayou."

"Mom?" Cayden asked, "you're not dying, are you?"

"Not even close," she said with a forced smile, trying

to breathe through pain so intense perspiration dotted her forehead and upper lip.

"Promise?" While Tristan searched for the nearest hospital on his phone, Brynn nodded to her son.

In under ten minutes, Tristan squealed to a stop beneath an emergency room canopy. "Hold tight," he said to Cayden. "Let me get your mom settled and I'll be right back."

"Okay…" Cayden sounded as if he was trying awfully hard not to cry.

After killing the engine, Tristan hopped out from behind the wheel, charging around the front of the truck to unfasten Brynn's safety belt and scoop her into his arms.

"I'm too heavy," she protested.

"How about letting me be the judge of that?"

Beyond thankful for his help, she rested her head against his chest.

Inside, nurses scrambled to get Brynn into a wheelchair, though she'd much preferred being held securely in Tristan's strong arms.

"Do you have your insurance information?" an admissions clerk asked.

"I-in my purse," Brynn managed.

"I'll get it," Tristan said. "I'll handle everything. You just focus on you."

Everything was happening too fast. The pain was too strong. Tears had started and showed no sign of letting up. The nurses wheeled her down an endless hall, farther and farther from Tristan and her son. The lights were too bright. The antiseptic smell too potent. "I— I'm going to be—"

A nurse fished a plastic bag from her pocket, holding it under Brynn's mouth. "There you go." She smoothed her hand up and down Brynn's back. "Try calming down. Everything's going to be okay."

"E-easy for you to say," Brynn muttered from between chattering teeth.

The nurse laughed and just kept on rolling to the maternity ward. "Hold on to that spunk, girl. You're going to need it."

CAYDEN FOUND A HIDING SPOT between a pop machine and wall. He sat there hugging his knees to his chest, wishing *really* hard his mom wasn't going to die. Coach Tristan kept promising she was gonna be okay, but Cayden was a first-grader and not stupid like a *littler* kid. All the grown-ups who'd come to the hospital—like their neighbor who'd told him to call her Miss Georgia, and Tristan's mom, Miss Donna—told him what his mom was going through was natural. But just like he wasn't stupid, he wasn't dumb, either, and all that screaming and crying coming from his mom's room couldn't be normal.

If his mom did die, then what? Was he supposed to run away? Or start looking for a new mom and dad?

Coach Tristan sat on the end of a sofa near Cayden's hiding spot. "Doing okay, bud?"

"No."

Tristan laughed, but instead of it sounding funny, like when he cracked jokes, it sounded kinda sad. "Me, neither."

He stood, stretched, then headed to the vending machines. "I need coffee and M&M's. Want anything?"

"Yeah. I want that, too."

Eyeing him funny, Tristan asked, "Your mom lets you drink coffee?"

"Yeah…" Cayden knew he wasn't supposed to, but

he lied. Just this once, if he drank grown-up coffee, maybe it'd make him feel more like a man. Because if he'd been a man when his dad died, maybe he could've done something to keep him alive. "I drink it *all* the time. Mom lets me have Snickers bars, too."

Nodding, Tristan said, "That's what I figured. Lots of cream and sugar in your coffee?"

"Uh-huh." Cayden wasn't really sure what that did to the coffee, but he'd heard people say it on TV, so it had to be good.

Once they had their food and shared the waiting room sofa, Tristan said, "I got a text a little while ago from Dominic's dad. They'll be here soon."

"That's good—I guess."

Helping Cayden unwrap his candy bar, Coach Tristan asked, "I thought you liked Dom?"

"I do." *But with Mom almost dying, I'd rather just sit here with you.*

Chapter Eight

Above all else, Tristan hated losing control.

Hours had passed since Cayden and Dominic had fallen asleep, folded like human origami into armchairs.

Sean had grabbed a Sudoku puzzle book before the gift shop closed, and seemed content enough. His pencil scratching against paper was the room's only sound outside of the occasional hospital PA announcement.

"How are you standing this?" Tristan asked, up on his feet to pace the same course he had all night.

Shrugging, Sean didn't look up from his page. "What are you keyed up about? Brynn's a great gal and all, but it's not like you really know her."

Not sure how to take his friend's casual assessment, Tristan said, "Guess you're right."

But was he? For whatever reason, however illogical it may be, Tristan did feel a certain closeness to Brynn. Whether it was the bond they'd formed during their trek through Lee Bayou or the fact that they'd both seen the end of their marriages, he couldn't deny caring.

Since both kids were zoned out, Tristan said, "I know you graduated a couple classes behind me and Jason and the rest of my crew, but you remember Mack, don't you?"

"How could I not?" He set down his puzzle. "The

guy was only the greatest thing to come from this town, like, ever—well, until the scandal."

"Keep this on the DL, but I'm guessing the whole reason Brynn went into labor early is due to a call she had yesterday afternoon from Ted Stevens, and—"

"Whoa—as in the baseball commissioner?"

"That's the one."

"Sorry." Sean shook his head. "Gonna take a sec to wrap my head around that one. Anyway, please continue."

Tristan explained how Mack had been on the good guy side of a sting operation, and now that all of the bad guys had finally been indicted, the commission was restoring Mack's halo. "The news hit her hard. Like the whole reason she ended up here was not only for the free house—but to escape the hatred of Mack's fans and their former friends. After weathering practically being run out of town by a lynch mob, owning nothing but a car and the clothes on her back, the commissioner now wants to host a special game in Mack's honor—with Cayden tossing a ceremonial first pitch."

"Wow..."

"Exactly. I don't even know what to say to her." Tristan resumed his pacing.

Glancing down the hall at Donna carrying a pink bundle, he said, "For the time being, looks like all topics are tabled. Our new friend Brynn had a beautiful baby girl."

CAYDEN STOOD IN THE CORNER of his mom's hospital room with his arms tightly folded, refusing to even look at the stupid baby everyone was freaking out about. She wasn't even cute, but all the grown-ups were talking in soft cootchie-coo voices and kept going on about her adorable tiny fingers and toes.

Dominic and his parents had left a long time ago, since his lawyer dad had to be at work today and Dominic had baseball practice. Cayden wished he could be at practice instead of in this stupid hospital with his stupid baby sister.

He snuck a look at her, cuddled in his mom's arms.

Coach Tristan stood at the head of his mom's bed, and he kept giving his mom and the baby a goofy smile— like he'd had too much beer or something. Miss Donna and Miss Georgia had gone home for a little while, but now they were back, along with a whole bunch of other ladies Cayden didn't know.

Nobody even looked at him.

He could just stand in the corner for the rest of his life, starving to death, and no one would even notice— especially not his mom who'd never once loved him as much as she now loved his stupid sister.

"Cayden," Tristan said, "how about me and you head down to the cafeteria for some scrambled eggs and bacon."

"I'm not hungry." Cayden refused to even look that way. He hated all of them for loving that baby and not him.

"Honey," his mom said, "please get something to eat. I know you had one of the cookies Miss Georgia brought, but I'd feel better if you at least had a little healthy protein."

"I don't even know what that is and anyway, even if I did, I don't want it!" He stormed past all the stupid ladies to go stand in the hall.

A few minutes later, Coach Tristan came out of his mom's room. "Got something on your mind?"

"No."

The hall was crowded with a bunch of people wearing blue and green doctor-looking suits. Lots of them pushed machines and wheeled carts and stuff.

"Well, that's good." Tristan put his hand on Cayden's shoulder, guiding him through all the crazy machine drivers. "Because I've got a ton of stuff I'd like to talk about. Plus, I'm starving. How about you just sit with me—I won't make you eat anything—and then you can give me advice on a couple things?"

"I s'pose that'd be all right."

"Cool. Bet you can't beat me to the elevator!"

WITH GEORGIA AND DONNA OFF at a Shreveport nursery they'd both been wanting to visit, and Tristan and Cayden sharing a late breakfast, Brynn finally had a moment alone to gaze at her baby in wonder.

Naming her Mackenzie had been a no-brainer. Even if the commissioner hadn't called, Brynn had wanted to honor the happy times she remembered with Mack. Now that she knew none of the horrible things she'd believed about him were true, that didn't mean a magical rewind button could be pressed. Former friends couldn't take back indescribably hurtful actions and words. Her mind's eye couldn't stop seeing the morning she'd woke to get the paper only to have the front yard literally covered in slime from thrown eggs. The entire town of St. Louis had hated her for Mack's actions and hadn't hesitated to show that hate in an assortment of creative forms.

The commissioner had seemed to think the fans would instantly forgive and forget, catapulting Mack's memory to its rightful position in baseball glory.

Brynn wasn't so sure…

Refusing to cry on this special day, she focused on the positives in her new life. Most especially the baby, her new friends and Tristan. He'd been a rock. Buying her dry clothing at the batting park, then finding her a hospital, always watching after Cayden. Considering the hard-line stance she'd taken on vowing to be independent, in the past few weeks she'd done a one-eighty. There was no way she could've pulled off Cayden's birthday party without help from Tristan and Vivian and Sean and even Miss Georgia. She even owed thanks to Coach Jason for letting Cayden on the team. Most of all, though, Tristan had made the most profound change in her life. How would she ever repay him?

Mackenzie opened her eyes and though Brynn had hoped her baby would have her daddy's dark hair and brown eyes, she had her mom's blue-eyes and the red hair to go along with them.

A knock sounded on the door. Tristan poked his head through. "Everyone decent?"

"We sure are." Her pulse raced just seeing his dear face.

"Cayden and I found a playground we'll be able to see from here, so I left him down there to work off steam. Hope that's okay?"

She nodded, guilty to feel oddly relieved. He'd been the only one not happy to meet Mackenzie. "How's he doing? He's never made it a secret he wants nothing to do with his baby sister, but the dark look on his face?" She shuddered. "He scared me. In the past year, I thought I'd been through just about everything a woman can, but this…"

"Give him time." Tristan cautiously approached the bed, skimming his hand over Mackenzie's red curls. "He's afraid you don't have enough love in you for two kids. And since everyone's making a fuss over the baby, he assumes she wins your heart."

"That's crazy."

"We both know that, but the kid's only a couple days past seven. Who really knows what's going through his head?" At the windows, Tristan said, "Seeing him out there playing, he looks like his usual self. With time, he'll come around."

"Hope so." She stared at her baby for a few seconds more, then to Tristan's strong back. Heat rose in her cheeks at the memory of him so effortlessly lifting her into his arms to set her in an E.R. wheelchair. The more she was around him, the more she really did believe he could do anything. Did that stem from his SEAL training or had he always been that way? Forcing a breath, she said, "I'm starting to sound like a broken record, but I really can't thank you enough for all you've done for me and Cayden. Especially last night, you were a godsend in the truest sense of the word."

He waved off her compliment. "Anyone in my position would've done the same. Shoot, the sanest thing for me to do would've been calling an ambulance."

Mackenzie had drifted off to sleep, her impossibly long eyelashes sweeping chubby cheeks. "No. The whole event was unsettling enough. Riding alone in an ambulance would've been too much. W-when I had Cayden, once he heard I was in labor, Mack never left my side. This time around, though Georgia and your mom and Vivian were sweet to stay with me, it was hardly the same. As crazy as it sounds, part of me wished for you to be in here, holding my hand for support."

He again stood beside her. "Why is that crazy?"

"I hardly know you. Yet, a part of me feels I've known you my whole life and…" Emotions got the better of her and silent tears streamed down her cheeks. "I don't even know what I'm saying. Everything feels out of control. Don't get me wrong, I'm thrilled Mackenzie's safe and healthy and I'll soon be back to my normal energy level, but that call from Ted Stevens threw me off balance. Just when I'd figured out how to live my life without Mack—hating him for all the horrible things he'd done—now I feel like Ted wants me to be the perfect grieving widow for the fans. No, his exact words were, 'I need you to put on a brave face for all of baseball.' Like if I could support what happened to my husband, then fans could put aside their disgust over the whole cheating scandal and get back to the business of filling seats. Buying beer and hot dogs."

Tristan took too long to reply. Was he thinking her a total nutcase? "You've said a lot about what this Ted guy wants, but Brynn, what do you want?"

"Honestly?" she laughed. "I just want to raise my kids in peace and never have to think of this whole sordid mess again."

"Then do it."

"You make it sound so easy. I thought I hated Mack, but now I'm not sure what I feel."

Then there's you... In such a short time, Tristan had done so much for her and Cayden—and now, Mackenzie. If he hadn't been there to help find her medical care, she hated to think what might've happened.

"Look..." His voice softened and he edged closer, as if he wanted to reach out to her, perhaps hold her hand. Instead, he held his respectable distance. Which made her irrationally sad. "Just my opinion, but I think you're asking an unreasonable amount of strength and mental clarity from yourself. You just had a baby. That's enough to keep any woman's emotions in flux for a damned long time. Before that, you lost your husband to a violent death played out in front of you at your own home. Toss in your forced move to Louisiana, all the crap Mack's sting operation put you through, and I'd say you're entitled to a nice, long nervous breakdown."

She laughed through silent tears. "You're so good to me. I can't imagine what your wife was thinking to have ever let you go." The moment the thought left her mouth, Brynn regretted it. "I'm sorry. The reason for your divorce is none of my business."

Though she'd have understood if he suddenly remembered an appointment for which he was late, Tristan didn't so much as flinch at her question. "No need for an apology. My divorce was my fault. Andrea couldn't take my lifestyle. I was never home and when I was, my body might've been with her, but my mind was already on my next mission. Back then, the action was like a drug. Only when I came home from a six-month stint in Afghanistan to find my house empty, save for a note on the counter, did I realize how much I'd taken for granted." Shaking his head, he stared out the window toward Cayden and his newfound playground friends. "Jack had only been two. Where he was concerned, I took Andrea's leaving as a wake-up call. I started spending a lot of time with him—tried making things right. With Andrea, too. But she wasn't having it." He shrugged. "By the time she decided to remarry, Jack and I were tight. Her decision to take him from Baywood—just twenty minutes north of my place in Virginia Beach—to California hurt me worse than her initial leaving. It finally made me understand the two of us never had what it took to go the distance."

Not knowing what to say, Brynn cast a faint smile. "On the flip side, Mack and I rarely ever argued, but look how that turned out. Maybe the real answer is some things just aren't meant to be?"

He sighed. "Guess so. Not that it makes any of it easier to bear." Leaning in close to the baby, he said in a silly voice, "Perfect beauties like you are who make life worth living."

"You've got all this time off," Brynn said, "why don't you go to Jack? Set up an official visitation schedule for his school holidays."

"Think Andrea would go for it?" Brynn hadn't known Tristan long, but the man she already respected didn't back down from anything. She hated this look of defeat that'd settled over him in regard to his son.

"Why wouldn't she? I can't imagine any mother who loves her child not wanting him to share a meaningful relationship with his father."

"I don't know…" He was back to staring out the window at Cayden. "We've got a break in the game schedule coming in a few weeks. Maybe I'll plan something then."

"I HOPE THIS ONE'S ALL RIGHT." Donna checked the buckles on the car seat she and Georgia had selected at a Shreveport baby superstore.

"It's perfect," Brynn said, finding herself yet again in the position of being indebted to virtual strangers for their kindness.

Tristan had fastened it into the backseat of his truck for the return trip to Ruin Bayou. Once there, she'd transfer the seat to her own car.

"What a gorgeous day this angel has for her first trek outside." Georgia hovered beside Tristan's truck, wielding a surprisingly hi-tech digital camera that she'd used since Mackenzie's birth to capture every burp and coo.

The weather was perfect. Clear skies without a breath of wind and temperatures in the mid-seventies.

Though a nurse had wheeled Brynn and Mackenzie outside, once the baby was settled in her carrier, Tristan insisted on helping Brynn into the tall truck to sit alongside her daughter.

"Cayden?" she asked her boy who'd hung back from the adults. "Want to sit back here with me?"

He shook his head. "I wanna sit with Tristan."

Though for safety, Brynn usually preferred Cayden be in the back, just this once, she figured he'd be fine. Maybe the treat of being up front with Tristan would make him feel special?

Donna took the two floral arrangements the garden club had brought, and Georgia held a plastic bag filled with Brynn's clothes and toiletries, along with a stuffed pink hippo Tristan bought in the gift shop.

With everyone finally in their vehicles and underway, Brynn realized she was exhausted, but in a good way. Having the baby early had again put her in the position of relying on others for purchasing the most basic of infant items. While she'd had the nursery set up for ages, Brynn hadn't even thought about the car seat or diapers or the multitude of creams and lotions needed for bath time and changing.

"Coach Tristan?" Cayden asked.

"Yessir?" Tristan stopped for a red light.

"Are we gonna practice hitting today? I missed team practice last night and don't wanna be bad at tomorrow night's game."

"I suppose we can play ball for a little while, but we need to help your mom and Mackenzie get settled first. You're the man of the house, and that means you've got a lot of responsibilities."

After glaring over the seat at the baby, he asked, "Like what?"

"Well…your mom's probably going to rest a lot the next few days. You should always make sure she has lots of juice and water to drink. You could probably make her snacks, too."

"I'll get Mom stuff," the boy said with a glower, "but I'm not helpin' that ugly baby."

"Cayden!" Brynn snapped. "Your sister is hardly ugly. What's got into you? You've been sour enough to have eaten a whole lemon tree."

"Leave me alone! I hate all of you!" Arms tightly folded, he turned his glare out the window.

"That's fine, but I happen to love you very much." Why, just when Brynn's life in general seemed to be looking up, was her son having a meltdown? With Tristan as an audience, Brynn was unsure how to handle her son's latest outburst. Planning to have a good, long talk with Cayden later, she now focused on more manageable issues. "Since I had Mac at a different hospital than planned and can't wait to see those bills start rolling in, does that mean I'll get a refund on the money I already paid?"

"I would think so." Tristan flashed her one of his gorgeous smiles in the rearview. "Want me to check into it?"

"No. But thanks. Pretty sure that's something I'll have to handle myself."

"Cayden," Tristan said, "we're not that far from town. Want me to drop you at school, or would you like another day with your mom and sister?"

"School. I hate that baby."

Brynn shared another look with Tristan. While the

commissioner's call may have lessened her immediate financial worries, where her son was concerned, she'd never been more afraid.

Chapter Nine

While Donna and Georgia hovered about Brynn and Mackenzie, Tristan stood on the fringes, feeling too big and incompetent. He tried thinking back to when Andrea had brought Jack home, but best as he could recall, he'd been sent to Libya only a few days after his son's birth. Sure, he'd missed the little guy and felt bad for dumping all the responsibilities of new parenthood on Andrea, but those fleeting moments of reality hadn't squelched his drive to tackle what at the time had felt more urgent. Taking down bad guys had been far more important than helping his wife change diapers or figure out water-to-formula powder ratios.

Earlier in the day, Vivian had stocked the kitchen with homemade casseroles, baked goods and snacks, as well as adorning seemingly every empty surface with bundles of pink balloons and flowers. A handmade Welcome Home, Mackenzie! banner had been hung lopsided over the front door.

Upon seeing it, Brynn's smile had been epic.

Tristan had fought a flash of jealousy.

Why hadn't he thought of making a sign? He wanted to be the one causing her happy glow. As much as his head rationalized the ridiculousness of that thought, he couldn't erase the fact that he wanted to be in Brynn's life. But why? What was it about her and her little family that made him constantly want to charge to her rescue? Or was it more about his own hang-ups about his badly fumbled past? Was he trying to prove he wasn't the total parenting and husbanding incompetent Andrea claimed him to be?

"This is all so pretty." Having left the sleeping baby upstairs, Brynn gave her friend a big hug. "How can I ever thank you?"

"No thanks necessary," Vivian assured. "That's what friends are for."

A shadow passed over Brynn's expression. "That's not what I experienced in St. Louis. The second they learned about what Mack had done, you'd have thought I carried his same shameful disease."

Vivian poured five glasses from the pitcher of freshmade fruit punch. "Sean told me Mack was cleared of all wrongdoing. That's wonderful. Maybe now, some of those old friends will apologize?"

"I'm not holding my breath waiting for that day to come. In fact, my plan is to carry on as if I never even heard from the commissioner." After sipping her beverage, she added, "Don't get me wrong, I'm thrilled my husband's name was cleared, but that does nothing to erase the damage already done to my heart."

"But you could have it all again," Vivian offered. "Just think, you'd be back in your mansion and getting invites to glamorous parties." A dreamy look settled over Vivian's features. "If I were you, I'd run to your former life."

But you're not Brynn. Tristan grew furious on Brynn's behalf. Vivian had no idea what those supposed friends had put Brynn through. Now here she was in Ruin Bayou making new friends, but judging

by Vivian, were any of them more genuine? Her trust
in every human kindness had been shattered, leaving
Brynn in what Tristan could only assume was a shell
of her former emotional self.

Tristan cleared his throat. "How about we all get out
of here and give Brynn her space."

"Sure you can handle everything on your own?"
Georgia asked, giving the new mom a warm hug.

"I'll be great, thanks. Really—to all of you, I can't
thank you enough for all you've done."

"Aw, it's been our pleasure." Donna was next in line
for a hug. "Like Georgia said, if you need the slightest
little thing, give me a call."

The two older women's sincerity caused tears of gratitude to well in Brynn's eyes. Vivian's words, Tristan
suspected, drew emotion from a deeper, more cynical
well.

With everyone on their way save for Tristan, she said,
"Who knew SEALs were also verbal warriors? Kudos
for a masterful job of sending Vivian on her way."

"She definitely falls under the category of With
friends like her, who needs enemies?"

Brynn chuckled. "I want to believe she means well—
look at all she did for Mac's homecoming. But does she
even listen to the words leaving her mouth?"

"Sometimes I wonder."

From over the baby monitor came a fitful cry.

Brynn shook her head. "And so it begins."

"While you take care of that cutie, I'm going to
switch the safety seat to your car. Where are your keys?"

"On the rack by the back door."

Completing his task, it occurred to Tristan just how
much he'd miss Brynn and Cayden and little Mackenzie if they did return to St. Louis. Which didn't make

much sense, considering it was high time he returned to his Virginia Beach base. He'd had his shot at family life and it'd been an epic fail. Now that Brynn at least had her memories of Mack restored to their former glory, she knew what it was like to lead an idyllic marriage. Tristan wasn't sure he'd ever known.

IT'D BEEN A WEEK SINCE Mackenzie's birth and Brynn felt physically stronger every day. Her emotions, however, were an entirely different story. Cayden's behavior was as gloomy as ever, and late night feedings were taking a toll. Those issues aside, she had a lot to be thankful for. Mackenzie's overall demeanor was sunny and once Cayden trudged onto his school bus each morning, Brynn settled the baby on a blanket beneath a gnarled-branch pin oak while tending the garden. Oftentimes Georgia would stop by for a chat, and Brynn had started very much enjoying the older woman's company.

Brynn now sat in the ballpark stands, heart racing as Cayden stepped up to bat. Even though the game was only for practice, she still battled nerves. He might currently be upset with her, refusing to believe she loved him every bit as much as his baby sister, but that hadn't affected her love for him one iota.

"What do you think of your brother?" Brynn asked Mackenzie, who sat staring wide-eyed in her carrier at her surroundings. "He looks handsome in his practice uniform, huh?"

Brynn looked forward to the time when her daughter not only smiled, but held at least a monosyllable conversation.

The night was pleasant. A light breeze kept away bugs. The scents of fresh-popped corn and hot dogs made Brynn's stomach growl. She asked her daughter, "Do you have a taste for salty, sweet or both?"

"I'm going for both," Tristan teased, "but what category do nachos fall under?"

"Hey, you." Seated on the end of the stands, away from the other parents, Brynn hadn't expected to see Tristan except for out on the field. "Why aren't you performing your coaching duties?"

"Oh—" his laugh warmed her through and through "—never fear. I'll be back to work soon. Just on my way to Jason's truck to grab a few more bats. Saw you and this beauty sitting over here alone and wanted to say hello. I've missed you Langtoines."

"We've missed you, too." And she had. As busy as Mackenzie had kept her, Brynn craved grown-up conversation.

"If you're up for company tomorrow night, think Cayden's ready for more batting lessons?"

"I'm sure he'd love it," she gushed—only not so much out of excitement for her son, but herself. Something about Tristan made her feel alive in a way she hadn't in a very long time. A thought that was both exhilarating and terrifying.

"Great. I'll see you guys tomorrow night. Six?"

"Yes. Great." Brynn prayed her voice didn't give away the fact that she felt like a teen facing her new crush. "Want to stay for dinner?"

"No," he said with a firm shake of his head. "But I appreciate the offer."

That once giddy tingle in her stomach? Firmly put in its place by reality. Tristan was no more interested in her than she should be interested in him. And really, what did she have to offer other than a wagonload of baggage? Considering he had the same, honestly, even if she was in the market for a new beau, there was no-where for their relationship to go.

"HOW WAS PRACTICE?"

Tristan walked in the back door to find his mother demolishing a bag of Oreos. "Aw, Mom, what're you doing? You've been awesome at your diet."

"I know." She handed him the bag. "But in my de-fense, it was your ex that drove me to them."

After tossing the bag in the trash, he asked, "What'd Andrea do?"

"She called about an hour ago—I guess she was re-turning your call? Anyway, I asked to talk to Jack and she told me he was in the pool and she didn't want him tracking water through the house."

"Sorry." He enfolded her in a loose hug, kissing the top of her head. "The reason I called her was to see when Jack's out of school. I want to see him. Wanna go?"

"You know it."

He left her to rummage in the fridge. Finding shaved turkey, he asked, "Want me to make you a grinder?" His official SEAL knickname was Grinder, given to him by his friends when after BUD/S training, he'd downed a good half dozen of the Italian sandwiches in an hour. "I'll hide veggies on it so well you won't even know they're there."

Sighing, she sat at the oak table. "I suppose. Do I get lots of ranch dressing on it, too?"

She might be his mom, but that didn't mean he couldn't shoot her a dirty look. "Since I want you with me for at least a hundred more years—no." He blew her a kiss.

"Was Brynn at Cayden's practice?"

"Sure was." Arms laden with lettuce, peppers and

a cuke, he said, "Little Mackenzie was with her, too. Man, what a pretty baby. She could be one of those kid models."

"Is Cayden adjusting any better to having a sister?"

"Not even a little bit." He spread mustard on a whole wheat roll. "I know it's not my place to step in, but I feel compelled to do something—at least out of respect for Mack."

"Hmm." Flipping through a stack of gardening and craft catalogs, his mom shook her head. "Ask me, what that boy needs is a father who'll give him a firm hand."

"Mom…" He set her sandwich in front of her before starting on a couple of his own.

"What? I'm only saying what everyone else in town is thinking. Cayden needs a father and you need a son."

"With all due respect, Mom, know what you need?"

She sweetly smiled. "More Oreos?"

"To mind your own business." Brynn had lost the love of her life to murder. The last thing she or her kids needed was for some guy who thrived in deadly combat to enter their lives.

BY MID-JUNE, MACKENZIE was growing like a weed and Brynn felt almost back to her usual energetic self. Cayden was still less than enthusiastic about his sister, but at least with school out for the summer, he'd given the constant glaring a rest.

Tristan came over most every night, helping Cayden with his hitting, and the work was paying off. In the Mud Bug's first game, Cayden had made it to first base. Unfortunately, the inning ended before he had the chance to score, but he was still pretty pumped. For the precious few smiles Brynn had seen on her son lately, she owed all of them to Tristan. She'd invited him to share their evening meal more times than she could count, but always, he had a ready-made excuse.

She'd just finished up that night's dishes and stood at the kitchen sink, watching out the window as her boy caught throw after throw. Tristan was so kind and patient with him. It pained Brynn to think how much his own son was missing by not having Tristan in his life. Sure, they'd soon share a visit, but visits weren't the same as sharing in a child's everyday existence.

With Mackenzie snoozing in her crib, Brynn carried the baby monitor outside, applauding Cayden's latest catch. "You're getting so good!"

"Thanks, Mom."

"When you guys are done," Brynn offered, "if you're hungry, I brought homemade cookies from today's garden club meeting. Georgia made them and they're not only fancy, but delicious."

"Sounds good." Tristan didn't let up with the action. To Cayden, he said, "Okay, bud, I want you to go farther out, that way you'll be able to catch any ball, anywhere on the field."

"Okay!" Cayden ran far past his fort.

Brynn tried focusing strictly on her son, but Tristan's shoulders and back as he wound up his pitches were a sight to behold. Then there was the sun-kissed strip of his neck just above his T-shirt collar. In full daydream mode, she wondered what it'd be like to step up behind him, wrapping her arms around him, pressing her hands to his chest, standing on her tiptoes to press her lips to the tantalizing bit of exposed skin. She could only imagine his intoxicating smell—sun and sweat and that extra, manly something that never failed to raise her pulse a few notches.

What are you doing? her conscience demanded.

For the rest of Tristan and Cayden's practice, Brynn's attention was solely on her son. But then Dominic rode up on his bike to play hide-and-seek in the fading light, leaving Brynn on her own with a man who she was almost ashamed to admit fascinated her.

"He's doing great." Tristan sauntered in her direction, setting her pulse racing all over again. As good as he looked from behind, his front view was that much better.

"I'm glad. Thanks again for your help."

He shrugged. "Got anything to drink?"

"Sure. What's your pleasure?"

"I'd love a beer," he said with a slow, sexy grin, "but I'm guessing since you're breastfeeding Mac, that's the one thing you probably don't have?"

Cheeks superheated, she nodded. "We do have apple juice, milk, fruit punch and that old standby, water."

He laughed. "Water will do—and some of those cookies."

"You got it."

He offered to help, but she directed him to one of the patio chairs. Upon her return she sat beside him, accompanied by sounds of the boys' laughter, the neighbor's sprinkler and plenty of singing crickets.

"You weren't kidding," he said after finishing his first cookie. "Georgia makes a mean gingersnap—loving the cream cheese icing."

"Told you."

After more strained silence, Brynn summoned the courage to blurt, "Did I do something to offend you? We used to talk a lot—and I liked that. Now you're here all the time, but I feel like you avoid me like the plague."

Setting his sweating glass of ice water to the patio table, he sighed. "I've been busy."

"Making plans to visit Jack?"

"And other things." They used to share such an easy camaraderie. What changed? Why did it matter?

"You've done so much for my small family. Is there anything we can do for you?"

On his feet, he paced. "It's no secret this town is brimming with matchmakers. I miss talking with you, too. But the last thing I want is for you—or your nosy neighbor—to get the wrong idea."

"Is that all?" She bit her lip not to laugh. "Are you afraid of ruining my reputation or the other way around?"

"You know what I mean."

"Sure. Vivian never fails to remind me how spectacular a male specimen you are…" The moment the words left her mouth, Brynn felt her cheeks heat.

As if he knew exactly how good his body was, he looked away and chuckled.

"Regardless, aside from Georgia and your mom, you're the first real friend I've made in this town and I don't want to lose you."

"I'm not going anywhere." But he was. Sooner than she'd like, he'd return to his Virginia Beach base. Then where would she be? Save for her children, once again alone. Which is what she thought she'd wanted. Now she wasn't sure. Raising one child on her own was tough enough. Two? Most nights she all but collapsed into bed, only to wake a few hours later to feed Mackenzie. But was surrendering herself to a man once again truly the answer? Besides which, Tristan had never even shown so much as an interest in kissing her, so why had these crazy thoughts taken hold now?

"Mom?" Cayden shouted from the fort.

"What, sweetie?" Tristan's gaze never left hers.

"Can I spend the night at Dom's? He called his mom on his cell and she says it's okay."

"Crazy, isn't it?" Tristan said. "Kids his age having their own phones."

"Mom? Can I go?"

"Sure, but be home early. Mackenzie has a doctor's appointment in the morning." Why, when her son and his best friend took off laughing down the block, was she suddenly jubilant, too?

"I should get going." Tristan gathered his glass and the napkin his cookies had been on.

"No." She took the items from him, in the process, grazing her fingers against his. The electricity was as undeniable as it was unwanted and unbelievably pleasurable.

"No?" Eyebrows raised, he blasted her again with his sexy-slow grin.

"Stay. Let's watch a movie or load Mackenzie into her stroller and take a walk." *I just don't want to be alone.*

"Sure." He hadn't budged and neither had she. The continued contact shimmered through her in delicious waves. "Although you do know when I'm not back at my mother's by eight, rumors are going to fly?"

She laughed. "Trust me, I've faced worse."

"That you have." Had she imagined it, or did he deliberately brush his thumb against hers? In the process, igniting cravings for more tantalizing complications than Brynn was equipped to handle.

Chapter Ten

What're you doing, man?

Tristan followed Brynn into the house, telling himself he wasn't checking out her new and improved behind. While she may have lost her baby bump, she'd kept the best of her curves. For all the denying he'd done regarding his attraction for Brynn, he struggled with the truth that had he met her under different circumstances, he might've made a play for her affections. But he'd had his shot at the whole family thing and blown it. She deserved more than he'd ever be able to give.

"Hungry for more than cookies?" she asked, looking far too pretty in faded cutoffs and a pink tank that accentuated full breasts. With her hair in braids, she looked fresh from his every naughty farm-girl fantasy.

He shook his head. "I'm sorry, but I really should get going."

"What's wrong?" she asked, voice raspy with what he could only guess was the same confusion dogging him. "You used to be the only person I could talk to—about anything. But ever since I had Mackenzie, you've been distant."

"Sorry." He drew out a chair at the kitchen table, turning it backward to sit astride, resting his arms on the railed top. "Truth is, with the baby, I feel awkward

being around you. Like you're some kind of saint someone like me has no business being around."

"You're kidding, right?" Hands over her face, she
shook her head.

"Hear me out. I'm getting antsy to get back on base.
Meanwhile, you're getting more firmly entrenched here
in Ruin Bayou. The two of us…" He shrugged.

"We can't be friends? Because that's all I'm asking
for."

He cocked his head. "Really?"

Everything about her flirty stance, from her full,
pouty lips to her heightened color, told him she was a
woman amenable to being kissed. Lord help him, but
Tristan was up for the job. But Brynn was hardly the
one-night-stand kind of girl he dallied with back in Virginia Beach. They knew up front he was only interested
in fun and were okay with it. He suspected Brynn, on
the other hand, didn't have a clue what she genuinely
wanted—especially in regard to him.

"Of course." Hands on her hips, she snapped, "What?
You think I asked you in for a booty call?"

"No." *Yes.* Was he so rusty with the fairer sex that
he'd totally misread her?

From over the baby monitor, Mackenzie cried.

Brynn said, "Be right back."

"I'll come with."

"Suit yourself." Miffed? Although why she'd be upset
with him, he wouldn't know.

In the nursery, sweet reminiscences did him in. At
this age, didn't matter if the child was a boy or girl, vis-
ceral memories raised an instant knot in his throat. The
scents of pink lotion and powder and baby shampoo.
His time with Jack had been so fleeting, he'd cherished
every bath and even diaper changes.

"What's up, pumpkin?" Lifting her baby from the crib and into her arms, Brynn's voice had grown intoxicatingly soft. "Hungry?"

Tristan found Brynn and the infant mesmerizing, especially so when Brynn settled into a rocker, tossing a fuzzy pink blanket over her shoulder to provide modesty while feeding Mackenzie.

He used to love watching Andrea feed Jack. When he'd been home, he'd stayed up with her late at night. Sometimes watching TV, sometimes quietly talking. Had Brynn shared the same memories with Mack? For reasons Tristan couldn't fathom, he didn't want to know.

Picturing Brynn with another man brought on an irrational jealous streak he had no right to feel, but it was there all the same.

When Brynn had finished, she changed the baby's diaper.

Before tucking Mackenzie back in her bed, Tristan asked, "Mind if I hold her a minute?"

Wordlessly, Brynn passed the infant into his arms.

Cradling Mackenzie to his chest, nuzzling the underside of his chin to her downy hair, he closed his eyes, breathing in her sweet, clean scent. Again, he was struck with an almost painful rush of emotions. He'd missed so much with his son. Great gulps of time he'd never get back. The worst part was, now that he realized the error of his actions, it was too late. Short of moving to California—out of the question unless he gave up the only life he knew as a SEAL.

Eyes welling, he swallowed hard, passing the sleeping baby to her mom. "Sh-she's gorgeous. You did good."

"Thanks." Once Mackenzie drifted off to sleep, they tiptoed from the room.

"Wow…" In the upstairs hall with the nursery door

closed, Tristan leaned against the wall, bracing his hands on his knees.

"You okay?"

"Yeah." He reinforced his lie with a firm nod. "I'm good. Guess I wasn't prepared for the kinds of memories holding sleepy Mackenzie would evoke."

"You held her at the hospital and seemed fine." Brynn ran her hand in warm, comforting strokes up his arm.

"That was different. This felt more like home. More intimate, you know?"

Nodding, she said, "I used to hate it when Mack was on the road when Cayden was this little. While in my head, I understand there are times a man—or woman—can't be with his or her child, in my heart, I don't like it. Cayden hated when his father was gone."

"How's he doing with Mackenzie? Any better?"

Brynn slid down the wall, sitting cross-legged alongside him. "I don't know. When he's with you or Coach Jason or his friends, he's a totally different boy than when he's with me."

"Still sullen? Resenting his sister?"

"Yep. He's got some crazy idea in his head that just because she's here, I love him less."

Tristan took a moment to mull that over. "Kids are weird. Strange things go through their heads—at least I know that was the case with me." He laughed. "He'll be all right. Just give him time." The advice was easy enough to give, but so far, what had time done for Tristan other than leave him infinitely more confused?

"This is delicious." Georgia tagged along with Brynn to Cayden's Saturday afternoon game. "Can't remember the last time I've had a hot dog."

"Save room for dessert," Brynn advised. "Cotton candy's the best."

Georgia nodded, smiling through her latest bite.

The weatherman and gray skies forecasted rain, but so far, it'd held off. Though the humidity was off the charts, at least they didn't also have to contend with blazing sun.

While her son looked adorable in his uniform, Tristan looked—whew, Brynn fanned herself with a magazine she'd found in her purse. His red Mud Bug jersey clung to him in all the right places and she appreciated both coaches following the tradition of wearing team uniforms. Nothing accentuated the male derriere quite like a pair of booty-hugging baseball pants.

"Did I miss anything?" Out of breath, Donna sat on the bleachers next to Brynn. Vivian hung with a group of team moms a little farther down. Mackenzie lounged in her carrier beside Georgia.

"Not yet," Brynn said. "Cayden's next up to bat. I swear if my heart beats any harder, I'll need CPR."

"Let's not go there," Donna urged. "I finally got to the doctor yesterday and he still wants me to lower my cholesterol."

"How's your weight?" Georgia asked. "I think you look great."

"Thanks." Donna blasted them with a smile. "I'm down twenty-two pounds, but the doc wants thirty more. Personally, I think I'm in more danger from starving to death than heart issues."

"Don't quit," Brynn said, surprising herself by giving the woman a spontaneous hug. "I'd like to keep you around a lot longer."

"Aw, you're a sweetheart—which must be why my

boy stayed at your house till after midnight last night?" She winked.

Brynn turned ten shades of pink.

Georgia snapped, "Donna Bartoni, I told you not to bring that up. Now Brynn's going to think I'm a snoop."

"Which you are," Brynn interjected.

"Sorry," Donna said without looking the least bit apologetic. "It's not exactly a secret I think Brynn and my son would make an adorable family. I'm excited to see progress is finally being made." To Brynn, she asked, "So? I'm assuming at some point during the night you two finally got around to kissing?"

Mouth clamped tight, Brynn covered her flaming face with her hands. Even worse than Donna's questioning was the fact that no, she hadn't gotten a kiss. Though she'd shamefully very much wanted one!

Georgia finished her hot dog and started on a bag of chips. "I'm taking all that silent blushing as a positive sign."

"Both of you hush," Brynn begged. "It's finally Cayden's turn to bat." Pulse hammering, barely able to breathe, she clenched her hands, praying he at least touched the ball with his bat.

"He'll do fine." Donna patted her leg. "Tristan says he's already come a long way."

"Strike one!" the ump called when Cayden missed his first pitch.

Brynn crossed her fingers and couldn't stop jiggling her right leg. "Come on, Cayden! You can do it!"

"Strike two!"

"Lord have mercy," Georgia muttered. "Come on, Cayden!"

On the third pitch, Cayden hit the ball so beautifully,

Tristan were only friends, didn't mean she couldn't look her best.

"Mom! Mom!" Cayden threw open the screen door. "I made a homerun!"

"That's awesome!" On her feet, she held Mackenzie on her hip while hugging him. "Tell me everything."

"Well, since it was only practice, Frank was pitching, and I just tried real hard to remember everything Coach Tristan taught me, and then *bam!* I hit it really, really hard and the ball went so far into the swamp, we couldn't find it and had to get a new one."

"Whoa…that's pretty cool." She looked over her son to Tristan, who'd helped make this miracle possible and mouthed, *Thank you.*

He mouthed back, *You're welcome.*

Maybe she was caught up in the fun of the moment, but she felt his words as clearly as if he'd whispered them in her ear. She imagined his breath, warm on her neck, and despite the day's heat she shivered. Something about the silent exchange struck her as intimate. And good. And she never wanted the feeling to end. "We should totally celebrate. Cayden, think we should invite Coach Tristan for a night of minigolf?"

"Yeah!" Her son jumped up and down. "*Pleeease,* Tristan! It'll be fun!"

All the excitement must've spooked Mackenzie, as she started to cry.

Cayden shot her a dirty look. "Stupid baby! Why you gotta ruin everything?"

"Hey," Tristan warned. "Not cool."

"Apologize," Brynn said.

"Why?" he sassed. "It's not like she's even smart enough to know what anyone says."

Pointing up the stairs, Brynn said, "Go to your room."

"But I thought we were playing minigolf?"

"All you're going to do is think about improving your attitude."

With Cayden in his room, having slammed his door behind him, Brynn finally exhaled.

Mackenzie still sniffled and her eyes were red, but she'd soon enough recover. It was her son who had Brynn worried.

Tristan put his hands in his pockets. "That could've gone better."

"Tell me about it. Welcome to my daily nightmare."

"What're you going to do?"

On her way to the sofa, she shrugged. "Beats me. Think I should take him to a counselor? He has been through an awful lot."

"True, but when he's with me, he's fine. My gut feel is that he's terrified of losing you to his little sister."

"But that's silly." Brynn placed Mackenzie in her play seat, then tidied to help settle her nerves. "How could he not know I love him? I tell him all the time."

"Want me to talk to him?"

"Would you mind?"

He flashed her a faint smile before charging up the stairs.

WHEN SOMEBODY KNOCKED ON HIS door, Cayden threw his batting mitt at it. "Leave me alone!"

The door opened anyway. But it was Coach Tristan and not his mom. "Can I come in?"

"I guess." Cayden sat crisscross applesauce on the bed. He knew he was too old for kindergarten stuff like that, but it made him feel better. Like back when he was little and everything was okay. His dad was still alive and his mom only had one kid to pay attention to.

"What's up?" Tristan sat on Cayden's toy chest.

"Nothing. I just hate my stupid sister."

Nodding, Tristan picked up the autographed baseball Cayden's dad had given him that'd been signed by most of the guys on his famous team. "I used to hate mine, too. There were a bunch of times she'd get a fancy dress or something girly like that and I wouldn't get anything. It wasn't fair. But now that I'm older, I get that girls need different stuff than guys. Right now, Mackenzie needs more because she's a baby. You had your turn to be the baby, but now it's her turn. As her big brother, your job is to help watch out for her and take care of her. But how are you going to do that if you hate her?"

Cayden shrugged. "Doesn't matter. Mom doesn't love me and she's gonna make me live in my pirate fort, because all she does is make stupid baby noises at Mackenzie."

Tristan studied the ball. "Sounds to me like you might be jealous. Kind of like I am of you having this awesome ball."

"Am not!"

"Just sayin'…"

"Well—" Cayden hit his pillow "—it's not fair Mom spends every second with the baby. What about me?"

"Do you know how many of your practices and games she goes to? Almost every one. And I'll bet all your baseball gear cost way more than Mac's diapers."

"I s'pose." Cayden didn't want to think about any of that. He just wanted to be right, because that's what felt best.

"And remember that awesome birthday party your mom threw for you?"

"Yeah," Cayden argued, "but you made my fort! She didn't love me enough to do that!"

"Okay, whoa." Tristan stood and he was so big he looked a little scary. "You need to knock it off. Back then, your mom could hardly cook you dinner, how was she supposed to build a fort? You know I think you're amazing, Cayden, but honestly? You're acting like a spoiled brat. I'm sorry you lost your dad—really, I am. He was an awesome guy. But that doesn't give you the right to go around being mean to your mom who loves you. If anything, you should be extra nice to her for all she does."

"You better stop or I'm going to hate you, too!" Cayden jumped off his bed and ran for the door, but Tristan caught him.

"No more running. You're going to stick around and face your problems like a little man."

"I hate you!" Cayden hollered, but then he was crying and hitting Tristan's legs, but even then Tristan didn't stop hugging him.

"That's okay," Tristan said. "If it makes you feel better to hate me, go right ahead."

Cayden cried worse than his baby sister and when Tristan still didn't stop hugging him, that made him feel good.

His bedroom door creaked open and his mom walked in. "Everything okay?"

He let go of Tristan to run to her. "I'm sorry," he said with a giant hug. "Please love me and don't leave me like Dad did!"

"Oh, sweetie, I will always love you. You mean the world to me."

"More than Mac?" He looked up at her and sniffed.

"It's different. Like when you get a new toy, it's fun. But that doesn't mean you don't still love your old toys just as much, because they've been with you the longest."

"Oh." Cayden kinda understood.

Tristan cleared his throat, then set Cayden's baseball back on the shelf. "I should, ah, probably get going."

"Already?" Cayden asked.

"I need to help my mom with some stuff. But you remember what we talked about and be good for your mom, okay?"

Cayden nodded. "I will." Rushing to his friend Tristan, he crushed him in a hug, too. "I love you. You're the most *awesome-est* coach *ever*."

"Thanks, bud. I think you're pretty awesome, too."

Chapter Eleven

I love you.

The whole trip to his mother's Tristan's stomach flamed with nerves. The last thing he needed was for an amazing kid like Cayden to put his trust and love in him, because clearly Tristan was lousy at being a dad.

He'd been trying to get ahold of Jack for a week, and always just missed him. Tristan was sick of Andrea giving him the runaround, and when he and his mom headed out there next week, he planned on setting some new ground rules. He'd been more than accommodating when it came to letting his ex run off with their son, but he'd be damned if she'd now keep him from even talking to Jack on the phone.

In the house, he found his mom in her crafting room, hot gluing rhinestones on a doll skirt.

"Rats," she said without looking up at him. "You're home way earlier than I would've liked."

"Please, stop with the matchmaking. It isn't going to happen—especially after what just went down."

He now had her undivided attention. "What did you do?"

"Nothing. Cayden was in a snit, so I offered to talk with him. He broke down and just when I finally felt like I'd broken into his shell, he goes and tells me he loves me."

"And that's a bad thing?" She sipped from her bottled water.

"Not just bad, but catastrophic. He's already lost his dad. If he's now looking to me as a father figure, that can't be good for him. I need to get back to my base. How's he going to handle two men vanishing from his life?"

She returned to gluing. "You know what my answer would be, so why are you even bringing this up?"

"Oh—" He laughed. "Let me run right out and buy Brynn a ring, resign from the navy and we'll all live happily ever after, right?"

"Works for me." She'd finished one doll skirt and started a new one. "I know just the right people to help with the wedding cake and flowers."

"Would you listen to yourself? You sound crazy. I already married once and when I made those vows, I meant them."

"Of course you did. But nothing lasts forever. Just like you never imagined Andrea leaving you, I never thought your father would be taken from me so young. But, honey, that's life. You have to grab happiness wherever and whenever you find it. I've seen the way Brynn looks at you and you look at her. Trust me, the fuel's already simmering. All you have to do is add a spark and *boom*. Fireworks—which reminds me, have you thought about asking her to be your official date for the Fourth of July?"

Tristan shook his head. "Did you find my secret beer stash? You sound tipsy."

"THANKS AGAIN FOR DOING THIS," Donna said at the Shreveport Regional Airport. "A week's parking would cost more than our whole trip."

"Aw, for all you've done for us lately," Brynn said, hugging Donna at the curb, "this was the least we could do, right, Cayden?"

He nodded, but looked near tears. "You're only gonna be gone a week, though, right, Tristan?"

"That's it, buddy." He ruffled Cayden's hair, then gave him a hug. "Think you can take care of things here while I'm gone?"

"Yeah." After a yawn—he'd fallen asleep in the car—he crossed his heart. "I promise to get your newspaper and mail every day."

"You're a good boy." Donna hugged him, too. "All right, we'd better get going. Georgia said the last time she visited her grandkids in Miami, it took a while to get through security."

Tristan teased, "That's because she probably talked the ears off of every person in line."

"Don't be fresh." Donna landed a smack to the back of his head. "Now hug Brynn and let's get going."

A feeling ranging between panic and anticipation ran rampant at Donna's suggestion. Though obviously, Tristan's chaste hold was purely for his mother's benefit, Brynn couldn't help but wonder what it would feel like experiencing the real thing. The closest she'd come was when he'd carried her into the hospital the night she'd given birth to Mackenzie. Brynn had to admit to having felt safe in his arms.

"Have a safe trip." On impulse, she pressed a kiss to his cheek. "I hope you have a wonderful time with Jack."

"Thanks." He held on longer than was probably necessary, but Brynn wasn't complaining. As if wanting to say more, his gaze searched hers, but then he released her, turning to Cayden, "Take care of your mom and sister, okay?"

"I will."

"All right, then…" Tristan grabbed his mom's suitcase. "Guess we're off. See you in a week."

What did it mean that Brynn already looked forward to picking him up?

"DAD!"

Tristan might be a big strong SEAL, but the sight of his son running toward him made his eyes sting like hell. "Hey, bud! Lord, I've missed you."

"I missed you, too!" After a long hug for his dad, Jack embraced his grandmother before taking them both by the hand, leading them across a wide, tree-filled front yard and into Andrea and Peter's ranch-style home. "Come see my room! And the pool! And Peter bought me an iguana! I named him Charlie!"

"I don't know if I'm brave enough to see that," Donna said.

"Come on, Grandma! He only bites if he's hungry."

She laughed. "Well, in that case, I hope you fed him today?"

"Yeah, I did." He opened the door, shouting, "Mom! Peter! They're here!"

The house was all right. Beige carpet, beige walls and comfortable leather furniture with colorful throw pillows. Oversize windows looked out on a backyard pool and on a fireplace mantel were too many pictures of family fun. Jack and Peter playing catch. Jack and Peter riding an amusement park roller coaster. Peter holding Jack's birthday cake while Tristan's son blew out his five candles.

"Tristan. Donna." Andrea approached from what he guessed was the kitchen. Peter was close on her heels. "How was your trip?"

"Good," Donna said. "Although I still miss the days of getting a nice meal on flights."

"Me, too," Peter said. "When I was a kid, all those little dishes fascinated me."

"Come on, Dad!" Jack tugged Tristan's arm. "I want you to see Charlie."

"Go ahead," Andrea urged. "Donna, you, too. Peter and I are just finishing up some appetizers for a small party we're hosting in your honor. We thought you might enjoy meeting some of our friends."

"Not really," Tristan said under his breath.

His mother elbowed his ribs. "That sounds nice. You two go ahead with your preparations and we'll have a nice visit with Jack."

Tristan had played with Jack and his pet for a solid hour, yet the whole day still felt surreal. As much as he loved his son, part of Tristan traitorously felt closer to Cayden. Every other word out of Jack's mouth was something to do with Peter, and Tristan's chest ached with loss. Oh, he'd always love his son with every breath of his being, but their relationship would never be the same. Tristan was man enough to realize Peter was doing a good job of surrogate parenting and for that, he was grateful. Peter hadn't been the ruin of Tristan and Andrea's marriage. For that, Tristan only had himself to blame.

That said, the main reason for this visit—aside from seeing Jack—was to follow Brynn's advice and make it clear to Andrea that he wasn't giving up on forging a meaningful bond with his son.

"You're awfully antsy tonight." Vivian used her phone's camera to snap a pic of Dominic on third base. For a Tuesday night, the Mud Bug's practice was running painfully long. "Missing your eye candy?"

Brynn adjusted the sunshade on Mackenzie's carrier. "What do you mean?"

"Don't act all innocent. You miss Tristan."

"I do not." Brynn could deny it all she wanted, but the truth was that she missed him and his mother. Which was silly. Aside from her rich fantasy life, she and Tristan had never shared so much as a meaningful glance. Or had they? And she'd been too wrapped up in single parenthood to even know?

Cayden's behavior had been a thousand times better since he and Tristan talked. Just one more way she was indebted to him. But was that the same as being attracted to him? It'd been so long since she'd been in the dating market, how was she even supposed to know?

"Then what's up with your jiggling knee? You usually only do it when Cayden's at bat, but tonight, you've been at it for two hours."

"Not that it's any of your business," Brynn said, "but I applied for a job today. I'm waiting for a call."

"Really?" Vivian leaned in closer. "I thought you were loaded now that Mack's name had been cleared? Why do you even need a job? Especially with a newborn?"

Where did Brynn start to explain? "I had wealth snatched away from me once and I don't trust it. If it's still there when it's time for the kids to start college, then great. Until then, the only person I want to depend on is me."

"I suppose that makes sense." Vivian fingered the lace trim on Mac's pink T-shirt. "But still, what're you going to do with this little angel? The cost of day care would eat whatever you make."

"That's what's so great about this job. I'd be working with Lindsay Brigham—you know? From garden club? I didn't know she owns Morgan Hill Nursery. Anyway, she said when her kids were little, she brought them with her, and she doesn't mind if I do the same."

Angling closer, Vivian asked, "So you've essentially already got the job?"

"There were three other applicants. Lindsay said she'd call tonight or in the morning."

"Good luck." Vivian's tone was sincere.

Twenty minutes later, Brynn's cell rang and it was Lindsay offering her the job. Brynn was excited, but one thing made the moment less perfect—the fact that she couldn't share her news with a certain special someone. Tristan.

"I ALREADY TOLD YOU, TRISTAN." Andrea jogged faster to try getting away from him. "Jack's too young to be flying cross-country. Either you come here or he doesn't see you."

Her attempt to outrun a SEAL was as ridiculous as her repeated efforts to sway him from his request. "And I told you, unless you want to go back to court, Jack is going to see me every other holiday and at least a month every summer."

"That's funny," she said without laughing as they jogged in place while waiting to cross a busy street. "With your schedule, how are you going to guarantee you'll be there for him next week? Let alone months in advance?"

She made a valid point, but he wasn't backing down.

His son was too important. Jack had to know no matter what happened between his mom and Peter, that his real dad—the one who'd cradled him the night he was born—would always be there.

"If you were even a little reliable," Andrea said, "I'd still be with you. But you're not, and I can't stand it. Never could."

"Then why the hell did you marry me?"

She broke down. "I loved you. But you loved the navy more."

He pulled her against him, holding her until she'd cried out her frustration. "For the record," he said into her hair, "I'm sorry. I never meant to hurt you. I just—I didn't know what else to do. A week after high school graduation I was a bluejacket and I've been a navy man ever since. I would do *anything* for my country, yet you treat me like I'm a deadbeat bum. Have I ever once been even a day late with child support?"

"No, but—"

"You're out of excuses, Andrea. Out of guilt I've let you call the shots, but no more. I've got a friend back in Ruin Bayou who lost her husband and her kid's a wreck. A boy needs his father."

"Jack has Peter."

Looking to the sky to keep from exploding, Tristan repeated, "A boy needs his *father*. We're going to set up a visitation schedule and if, for whatever reason I have to tweak it, I'd appreciate your cooperation. There are lots of navy wives out there, Andrea, who make their marriages work despite deployment. I'll take half the blame for our relationship falling apart, but I'm done accepting it all."

"YOU EXCITED?" BRYNN ASKED Cayden Saturday afternoon on the way to the airport to pick up Tristan and his mom.

"Uh-huh. Do you think Tristan will be able to go to tonight's game, or is he gonna be too tired?"

"I think he'll manage." At least she hoped so. Not only couldn't she wait to hear how his visit with Jack and Andrea had gone, but she had her own news about her job.

They made it thirty minutes early, so they looked at all the local artwork, then found a comfy seat and people-watched, taking turns guessing where arriving passengers had been.

Finally, Tristan and Donna's flight arrived and Brynn's pulse raced like that of an excited child on Christmas morning.

"Tristan!" Cayden didn't have to hide his enthusiasm. He ran to his friend, nearly knocking him down from the force of his hug. Brynn envied her son, wishing she could do the same. Instead, she settled for a smiling, welcome-home hug first from Donna, then from Tristan.

"I missed you," he said low enough for her only. Had she imagined it or had his hold been stronger than when he'd left? His lemony aftershave acted like an aphrodisiac. She'd forgotten how heavenly he smelled.

"I missed you, too," she admitted, shyly ducking her gaze. She wanted so badly to hold his hand on the way to get his luggage, but Cayden had already stolen the honor. She couldn't be too disappointed, though. Her son's happiness had always come before her own, but just this once, she wouldn't have minded stealing some for herself.

Donna chattered away, but Brynn had a tough time concentrating on what she was saying.

While Cayden helped drag Donna's bag off the conveyer, Brynn hung back with Tristan, wanting to say so much, but in the end, saying nothing at all.

"You got anything going on tonight after the game?"

"As a matter of fact," she joked, "I'm invited to what I hear is going to be a wild party."

His expression faded. "For real?"

"No." She laughed. "I'm hardly the party type. I was teasing."

"Oh." For a highly intelligent man, he seemed to have a tough time asking, "I was thinking that after the game you and I might grab a steak at Scooter's. Is there any way Cayden could stay with Dom?"

"I—I'm sure Vivian won't mind. I'll ask if she'll watch Mac, too." Was this an honest-to-goodness date he was asking her on?

"Good. This isn't a date or anything. Just thought it might be nice to catch up."

If Brynn's excitement had been a balloon, it would've popped. Whatever. She hadn't even wanted to go on an official date with him.

Oh, yes you did, her conscience begged to differ.

ALL TRISTAN HAD WANTED THE whole time he'd been gone was to talk to Brynn, so now that he finally had her to himself, why did he feel like a tongue-tied teen? Vivian had taken Cayden and the baby so Brynn could ride with him to the restaurant. During the meal, just when he thought he might be able to open up about how he really felt in regard to so many things—Jack, his failed marriage and even his unwanted crush on her, his brain shut down.

Now, in the restaurant parking lot, seated in his truck,

Brynn looked so pretty in the dim light, he was especially off his game—if he'd ever even had one.

"Why aren't you starting the engine?" she asked, her voice the soft haven he'd craved for seven days.

Abandoning the keys in the ignition, he turned to face her. "Look, I'm apparently really bad at this, so I'm just going to come out and say it. I missed you—like, *really* missed you. I wanted to tell you my time with Jack was beyond amazing. We surfed and went to Disneyland and Universal Studios and more than that, we got the chance to really talk about how he's doing." He swallowed hard, remembering how grown-up Jack had seemed for a kindergartener. But then Cayden was the same. Just when Tristan was coaching him and thought the kid didn't have a clue where he was coming from, Cayden far exceeded Tristan's expectations. "He's good. And he doesn't hate me like I feared."

"I could've told you that." Brynn reached across the seat, covering his hand, filling him with yearnings he had no right to have. "If anything, my guess is you spend far too much time hating yourself. Wondering what might've been, when all that happened with Andrea is in the past. Right now, you have to look forward. Figure out what's best for not only Jack, but you."

"You make it sound so easy." Tristan's chuckle was strained. Her hand was still on his and more than anything, he wanted to lift it to his mouth, kiss the skin he already knew to be unbearably soft.

"You and I both know when it comes to relationships, nothing's easy. I thought after losing Mack, I'd never even want to try again, but lately—especially when you were gone, I, well…" She bowed her head and smiled shyly, in the process, spilling ginger-red curls across her face.

Pulse erratic, not sure if he was breathing at all, Tristan summoned his every ounce of nerve to tuck her hair behind her ear, then cradle her cheek. "You're so beautiful."

She shook her head. "I have too many freckles and my nose is funny."

"I adore your nose," he stupidly admitted. "And damn near everything else about you."

"Stop..." Her shimmering eyes told him to go on.

"With everything in me, I want to kiss you."

She licked her lips. "What's stopping you?"

"The fact that I'm running out of time. Eventually, I have to get back to my base. Then what? You and Cayden and Mac have made a great life here—I know, because I remember how simple and sweet small-town ways used to be."

What if you stayed? her penetrating stare asked. Or was it his own wishful thinking?

"What if I don't care? What if I want to know if what I've been curious about for all these weeks is even worth my while?"

"You've been curious about me, huh?"

She nodded. Edged closer on the seat to rest her head on his shoulder. Her silky curls caressed his neck, fueling forbidden images of her riding atop him, those curls playing hide-and-seek with full breasts.

When she looked up, it would've been so easy to kiss her. To tug her onto his lap and do more. But what kind of man would that make him?

Honestly? His need for her had become damn near impossible to deny. She deserved better. And he wasn't just talking about the fact that his divorce had made him damaged goods, but because his career left precious little room for a meaningful private life. He couldn't do that to her—or himself. Start something special he'd never be able to finish. Which was why he cleared his throat and said, "We should probably get going."

Chapter Twelve

"You've got to be kidding," Vivian said the next morning while Brynn fed Mackenzie. Sean was still sleeping and the boys were already playing cowboy in Dominic's tree house. "I thought SEALs were the ultimate good time guys, but you two were on the verge of kissing and *he* put on the brakes?"

"Yep." Shaking her head, Brynn sighed. "But the thing is, he made a good point. What's the sense in either of us falling for each other when he's leaving? Cayden's already hopelessly attached. He's going to be shattered when Tristan returns to duty. I can't begin to figure out how to make that okay. So why would I want to have myself torn by his leaving, as well?"

"I suppose…" Vivian sipped her coffee. "But hey, at least you finally admitted you have a thing for the guy."

"Do I?" A hot blush traveled all the way to her toes. Laughing, she admitted, "Yes, I do."

"Well, you know he's at least going to be in town until the end of baseball season. What if you gave things a trial run and it turns out so great he asks you to return to Virginia Beach with him?"

"Are you listening to yourself? We haven't even kissed, and here you've got us marrying?"

"I didn't say anything about tying the knot," Vivian said with a wicked wink. "For starters, you could just shack up."

DURING SATURDAY'S MUD BUG GAME, from his position behind first base, Tristan had a perfect view of Brynn—not a good thing considering the calico sundress she'd worn fluttered in the light breeze, giving him teasing glimpses of her bare legs. She'd forced her unruly curls into flirty pigtails and her lips looked more full—had she changed her lip gloss? The fact that he'd even noticed such a thing was a bad sign.

He needed to focus on Cayden, who was up to bat.

Come on, bud. You can do it.

"Strike one!" the ump called.

"Hit it hard, baby!" Brynn called from the stands.

The pitcher threw again and Cayden missed again.

Tristan's stomach couldn't have been queasier than if he'd been at bat himself. *Come on, bud. Remember all you've learned. I know you can do this.*

For his last pitch, Cayden's hold on the bat was just right, as was his stance. Tristan also liked the boy's fierce look of determination—reminded him of the old days, playing with Mack.

"Foul ball!" the ump said of the next pitch.

Tristan's gaze strayed to Brynn. She held Mackenzie on her lap and had her fingers crossed.

The pitcher wound up…

"You can do it," Tristan said under his breath.

Cayden hit the ball, but it was too low and slow, resulting in an easy catch for the opposing team.

"Out!" called the ump midway through Cayden's run to first.

"Good try," Tristan told the scowling boy. "Next week, we'll work on your strength and speed."

"Okay…"

A glance in the stands showed Brynn was also disappointed. More than anything, Tristan wished for the power to make all three Langtoines smile.

MONDAY MORNING, BRYNN HAD BEEN at her new job for only a couple hours when Donna and Georgia appeared with Tristan in tow. Didn't take a rocket scientist or a gardening expert to see the situation was yet another attempt to steer the two of them together.

"Looks like Mackenzie's hard at work." Donna leaned over the portable playpen Lindsay had let Brynn set up. The baby rested on her back in dappled sun, staring intently at the fragrant honeysuckle vines dangling over her head.

"That's why she gets the big bucks," Brynn teased.

"I wonder if you could help me pick out a few azalea bushes," Georgia asked. "I'm wanting to put them at the back of my new bed. By the pines. But I want red and all I can find are white."

"If you and Donna wouldn't mind keeping an eye on Mac for a few minutes, I'm pretty sure I remember seeing some in one of the back houses."

"Perfect," Donna said. "Tristan, you go with her. She shouldn't be doing heavy lifting."

He shook his head, mumbling, "Obvious much?"

"Go on," Georgia urged Brynn. "And be sure you're good and thorough. If Lindsay comes out, we'll tell her you're doing a great job."

"Sorry about that," Tristan said as they made their way down a winding gravel trail. "Mom's got it in her head we're a couple."

"It's okay." Though Brynn knew she shouldn't want to be in a relationship with Tristan, try telling that to her body. The path was narrow, meaning every few seconds her bare arms brushed against his. The day was already warm and occasional overspray from the sprinklers provided temporary relief.

"Not really." He held out his arm to stop her beneath an arbor heavily draped with wisteria. "Because truthfully, I can't stop thinking about what it might be like if we were…you know, maybe more than friends. But that can't happen, right?"

"It can't?" she dared ask. The confined space pressed their bodies perilously close. Close enough for her to smell morning coffee and maybe a trace of sweet cinnamon on his breath. More than anything, she wanted him to throw caution and worry to the wind and kiss her as if there was no tomorrow. Because in her experience with Mack, she'd discovered that in a heartbeat, all you knew could be ripped out from under you, resulting in emotional ruin. "Or, you won't let it happen?"

"Brynn…" His voice was raspy as he leaned in close enough that barely a leaf could've passed between them. "Lord, woman, you make me crazy."

"Likewise…"

"So what do you want to do?"

Heart pounding, she wondered if she'd ever met such a clueless man. Duh? What did he think she wanted him to do? *Kiss me, you big, gorgeous oaf.*

"Got something to run by you," Tristan said to Jason as they put up equipment after Tuesday night's practice.

"Shoot." He hefted the net bag holding the bases into the bed of his truck.

"Not sure if you noticed, but Brynn Langtoine and I—"

"Hold it right there. Hate to break it to you, man, but everyone in town's noticed. We could get a betting pool going on when you're finally going to make your move."

"That's just it." Tristan loaded the spare bats. "At the end of the season, I'm heading back to Virginia Beach. Why start something I can't finish?"

"Who says?"

"My common sense." Leaning against the side of the truck, Tristan tried explaining. "Let's say we hook up. Then what?"

"You'll never know if you don't at least ask her out."

"I did. We hit Scooter's the night I got back from Cali, but it turned out to be an epic fail."

"Mind giving me a hand with this?" Jason nodded to the rolling cooler they kept filled with bottled water and Gatorade.

"Sure."

With the cooler lifted in place, Jason asked, "What could go wrong over a nice steak?"

"Essentially, me." *What am I even looking for?* Last thing he wanted was for Brynn to feel as though she and her kids were just stand-ins for the family he'd lost.

"What'd you do?"

"That's just it. Nothing."

Jason jingled his keys. "Man, hate to break it to you, but you've got issues. Brynn's a great gal. If you're even thinking of starting something with her, you need to be sure where you stand."

"Like marriage?" Tristan coughed. "Can't. Already tried and failed."

Climbing in his truck, Jason said, "With an attitude like that, I see why…."

AFTER WORK FRIDAY, BRYNN AND Donna helped Georgia plant her new azaleas. Though the day was warm, thick cloud cover kept the temperature in the eighties as opposed to the usual nineties.

Mackenzie lounged beneath pines on a nearby blanket while Cayden played at Dominic's.

They'd put in six of the dozen plants when Donna sat back on her heels, rubbing her left arm.

"You okay?" Brynn asked.

"Sure. I've just felt out of sorts all day." She rubbed her chest. "Indigestion. Probably from the vegetables Tristan's been pushing."

"Never have liked them," Georgia said. "Especially not Brussels sprouts." She blanched. "Just saying the name makes me nauseous."

Brynn laughed. "Cayden feels the same."

The three women worked in companionable silence, finishing the planting, then fertilizing and spreading fragrant cypress mulch.

"Y'all are a godsend," Georgia said once they stood back to admire their work. "This would've taken me a week under my own steam."

With her arm around Georgia's shoulders, Brynn gave her friend a warm squeeze. "You'd have done the same for us. But now that we're done, how about some of your sweet tea?"

"You got it."

Brynn lifted Mackenzie, swooping her high for a kiss. "You're so pretty."

The baby cooed.

With Mackenzie on her hip, Brynn shook pine needles from the blanket, then slung it over her free arm. Only then did she notice Donna slumped against one of the patio chairs.

Running to her, she asked, "Donna? You okay?"

She nodded, but it was obvious from her crooked stance that something was off.

Taking her cell from her back pocket, Brynn found it dead.

"Hang tight," she said to Tristan's mom. "I'm going to call 9-1-1 from Georgia's house phone."

Donna shook her head. "I—I'm…" Before finishing her sentence, she'd crumpled to the ground.

TRISTAN PACED IN THE O.R. waiting area. Though his mom's doctor assured him she'd had *only* a small blockage, he wouldn't feel better until seeing her for himself.

"She'll be okay," Brynn said. She'd been a lifeline for him all afternoon, helping him through not only his fear, but mountains of hospital paperwork. Georgia had stayed behind, volunteering to watch Mackenzie for as long as necessary. "You know your mom. She's too stubborn to stay sick for long."

"You got that right."

Cayden sat small and quiet in an oversize chair, playing with his 3DS game. Of any of them, he'd had the toughest time with Donna's hospitalization. According to Brynn, he and Dominic had been riding their bikes when the ambulance came.

They'd watched as paramedics administered CPR.

Brynn said he'd had a meltdown, remembering a similar scene with his dad, only with a more horrific ending.

Tristan went to him now, acting on instinct when he lifted the boy into his arms for a hug. "Thanks, bud, for helping my mom get here safe."

The boy nodded, hiding his face in the crook of Tristan's neck. "I was so afraid she was gonna die."

"I know. Me, too, but the doctor and your mom say she's going to be much better soon."

"Promise?" Tristan hated like hell making that kind of promise to a kid who'd already lost so much, but for Cayden's sake, and his own, he nodded.

"Absolutely. By this time next week, she'll be all better."

Brynn wrapped her arms around them both and in that moment, Tristan experienced a crystalline clarity as to what he needed to do. Brynn and her son and daughter had become like family to him. He'd be as lost without them as he would his mom, which was why he vowed from this moment on to put aside his fears for what the future might hold and instead, embrace the infinite possibilities.

"WOULD YOU ALL QUIT FUSSING over me," Donna complained three days later while Tristan fluffed her pillows and Brynn placed a bowl of homemade chicken noodle soup on her bedside table. "The doctor says I'm fit as a fiddle."

"Correction." Her son perched on the edge of her bed. "You will be in four to six weeks. Until then, you need to take it easy and eat."

"I'm not hungry."

"Your home care pamphlets say that's normal." Brynn tapped the papers that were also on the nightstand, though she hardly needed to look as she'd learned them by heart. "But try eating at least a little something to keep up your strength."

"If I eat will you all leave me in peace?"

"Maybe." Brynn clinked the spoon against the side of the cranky patient's bowl.

From the living room, Mackenzie cried.

"Go ahead," Tristan said. "I'll take care of Mom."

Brynn jogged toward her crying child, only to stumble across an enchanting scene. Sticking to the hall's shadows, she watched Cayden carefully take Mackenzie from her carrier.

"Shh…" He gave her a light jiggle. "You have to be good so Mom can help Miss Donna feel better."

The baby cast a wide-eyed stare at her big brother, in the process, melting Brynn's heart, giving her one more reason to be indebted to Tristan. Without him, sure, Cayden would've one day learned to love Mackenzie instead of resenting her, but it might've taken twice as long.

"She likes you," Brynn said to her son.

"I guess." When Mackenzie whimpered, he jiggled her more. "Tristan says I need to help you and I figured whenever she's crying, she usually just wants someone to hold her."

"That's very smart of you."

"Thanks." His smile warmed her through and through.

"Everything good in here?" Tristan asked.

"Yeah." Cayden sat on the sofa, holding his sister upright on his lap. "Mac just needs a lot of attention. I'm glad I'm not as spoiled as her."

Brynn and Tristan shared a laugh.

LATER THAT NIGHT, CAYDEN WAS having a sleepover with Dominic, and Brynn was feeding Mackenzie in his mother's living room when Tristan asked from the hall, "Mind if I join you?"

"Sure." She repositioned the baby to her other breast, preserving her modesty with the infant's blanket. Brynn's beauty never failed to stir him. When she held her perfect daughter, the duo did him in.

"Mom's finally sleeping." He eased into his father's old armchair, rubbing his aching neck. "I swear, I've had friends with massive bullet wounds more cooperative than her."

Brynn laughed. "She's for sure keeping us on our toes."

He looked at his hands, then her. "Again, I can't thank you enough for your help."

"Then maybe we're finally even for all you did for me when I still carried this one."

"Fair enough," he said with a weary chuckle. Leaning forward, resting his forearms on his knees, he sighed. There was so much more he wanted to say to her, but wasn't sure how.

"What's with the sigh? Still worried about your mom?"

He shrugged. "Now that she's out of the woods, I'm more bugged by you."

"Me?" Her eyebrows raised. "What'd I do?"

"For starters, you have adorable hair and freckles."

She wrinkled her smallish, straight nose. "They're awful. No matter how hard I try, I can't cover them up."

"I would never want you to."

"Have you been drinking?" she asked with an indecipherable smile.

"Not a drop—though a beer might help me sound a hell of a lot more eloquent."

"O-kay…" Mackenzie had fallen asleep. Brynn slipped her out from under her blanket and placed her in her carrier before buttoning her own blouse.

His mouth had gone dry at the prospect of his upcoming admission. "Fourth of July is next week and this town does it up right. I know I said I didn't think we should initiate anything romantic, but with Mom getting sick, I—" He looked down. "Well, I reassessed a lot of the bull I've been shoveling. Bottom line, I think the world of you and Cayden and whatever time I have left in town, I'd very much enjoy spending with you. Which leads me back to the Fourth. Want to be my official date?"

Chapter Thirteen

Brynn honestly wasn't sure what to say. She'd like nothing more than to be Tristan's date. But she was also a huge fan of self-preservation, and playing with him was akin to setting off fireworks in the palm of her hand—dangerous where her heart was concerned.

"So your answer's no?" He'd hardened his jaw.

"I didn't say that. It's complicated." Mimicking his pose, she leaned forward, too. "I'm a single mom with two kids. Last thing I need is a one-night stand or just fooling around. For me, that boat sailed a long time ago. If we go out, I need to know you're not just toying with me. That there's at least a chance of you one day feeling more, which I know is a fairly ludicrous request when all you're wanting is to attend a town picnic and parade."

"Actually," he said, "I appreciate your honesty. And for what it's worth, Brynn Langtoine, since the day I first saw you, you've fascinated me. No matter what, looking at you now, I can't for the life of me imagine that fascination fading anytime soon."

THE MORNING OF THE FOURTH brought rain, thunder, hail and high winds, but by the parade's noon start time, the sky was a clear, perfect blue. The storm had left behind cooler temperatures and at least temporarily, the seemingly omnipresent Louisiana humidity was gone.

Brynn took special care with her navy-and-white-plaid dress. She'd wanted to try straightening her hair, but her curls weren't having it. In the end, she settled for a festive updo with plenty of trailing tendrils. While applying her makeup, she couldn't help but smile at the notion of Tristan finding her freckles pretty. After adding white sandals, she chased down Cayden in his fort to make him change into the special edition holiday T-shirt all the local businesses had been selling. The proceeds would help build a new elementary school playground.

"Aw, Mom," Cayden complained when she even went so far as to make him wash his face and hands. "How come Mac doesn't have to do all this work?"

"Because she wasn't silly enough to get dirty right before she knows Tristan's coming."

"Oh." Brynn followed him to the bathroom to supervise and brush his hair. Finished, he said, "Dom told me he heard his mom and dad talking about how Tristan told Coach Jason that you and Tristan are going on a date today. Is that true?"

Suddenly flushed with anticipation, she nodded. "Not that it's any of your beeswax."

"Are you gonna kiss him?" Instead of making an icky face like she would've expected, he cast her a hopeful smile. "Because if you do, then Dom says you gotta get married. And that's good because Tristan would have to be my dad, right?"

Her anticipation turned to apprehension. "Sweetie, just because we're going on a date, doesn't mean anything special. I mean, it's special because it's extra fun, but that doesn't have anything to do with getting married. In fact, you need to know that probably won't happen. Probably when baseball season's over, Tristan's going back to work in the navy."

"No, he won't." Cayden raised his chin. "I told him I love him and I know he loves me, so once he loves you and Mac, he's *never* going to leave."

BRYNN WISHED SHE COULD IGNORE the pang Cayden's statement created in her chest, but instead it served as the catalyst to get him professional help ASAP. Odds were, Tristan was going to leave, and when he did, what kind of hole would that create in her son's already fragile heart? Even as an adult, Brynn wasn't immune to Cayden's brand of fear. How could she enjoy her day with Tristan if the whole time she was with him, she only focused on the question of when—or even *if*—he was leaving?

How? By sheer will she was determined to put aside nagging worries in order to make this day special for not only her kids, but herself.

Walking down the street with Tristan, Cayden riding his shoulders while she pushed Mackenzie's decorated stroller to find the perfect position to watch the parade, it occurred to Brynn that this was the first time she'd been able to relax and enjoy herself as opposed to being part of the spectacle. As Mack's wife, she'd usually been assigned a special place to sit and had to make small talk with local and regional bigwigs. Not that she'd minded, but it was nice just being part of the crowd.

"What do you think?" Tristan asked Cayden in front of Bell Shoes. "Does this look like a good spot?"

"Yeah!" Cayden clapped to see the Ruin Bayou High School band already marching down the street. "Hey—just like in that 'Yankee Doodle' song, they have feathers in their hats!"

Brynn and Tristan laughed.

"Cool! Look!" Cayden pointed up at an airplane with a banner streaming behind it. It said Happy Fourth from D-Shawn's Lumber! "That's the coolest thing ever!"

"Sure is…" Tristan was staring, too.

Funny, but all Brynn had eyes for were her two handsome men. The two of them got along so well. Sometimes so well, she felt she should pinch herself in case she might be dreaming.

As float after float passed and beauty queens and Shriners in their tiny cars, Cayden had not only filled his pockets with candy and Mardi Gras-style beads, but Tristan had filled him with cotton candy and popcorn.

When one particularly noisy float passed, Mackenzie was spooked, but Brynn held her and soon she'd returned to her usual wide-eyed staring.

"Having fun?" Tristan asked her when a troop of baton twirlers sashayed by.

She nodded. And when Tristan held out his hand, she eased her fingers between his. The happiness in her stomach was akin to lightning in a bottle. After months of darkness, she'd finally stepped into dawn and the sensation was unlike anything she'd experienced before.

Tristan lowered Cayden to his feet. "Hey, while I'm thinking of it, I want a picture of the three of you."

"Yay!" Cayden was all too happy to ham it up.

Brynn took Mackenzie from her stroller, holding up her little hand in a goofy wave.

Tristan had his phone ready. "Smile and say 'cheese…'"

"Cheese!" Brynn's son gave new meaning to smiling for the camera.

From the parade, they went to a town-wide barbecue, feasting on pulled pork, roasted corn and watermelon.

More tables were laden with a myriad of potluck salads and desserts.

Before the fireworks, Tristan called his mom, who was home with Georgia in the air-conditioning. Upon confirming she was doing fine, they moved on to watch hilarious homemade raft races on Turtle Lake.

By the time the ice cream-eating contest ended with free all-you-can-eat sundaes for all, Brynn was not only stuffed, but exhausted.

"I don't know about you," she said to Tristan, "but Mackenzie and I are ready to claim our spot for the fireworks and just chill."

"Sounds like a plan."

"No!" Cayden hopped side to side. "I wanna play with my friends."

Since most of the baseball team was horsing around on the park's playground, Brynn said, "All right, but don't go anywhere else."

"Thanks, Mom!" He ran off.

"This look okay?" Tristan asked Brynn when he found a grassy mound in the shade.

"Perfect."

While she took Mackenzie from her stroller and made a quick diaper change, Tristan spread the blanket they'd stashed in the lower basket of the baby's ride. By the time she finished, he'd already stretched out, lying on his side.

Brynn followed suit, resting Mackenzie between them. "I didn't know how tired I was until now."

"No kidding. But it's been a good day, huh?"

"It really has. Thank you." Their gazes met over Mackenzie. There was a heat behind his stare she hadn't seen before. A contagious energy that had nothing to do with physical strength. More like an emotional high. "I know Cayden's had a ball."

"I'm glad." He stretched his arm toward her with his fingers tracing her cheek. "But he's easy. You're the one I've been trying to impress."

"You've been trying, huh? Like you orchestrated the whole town to make sure I had the best time?"

"Exactly." He toyed with her hair. "It cost my entire fortune to pay everyone to host a quintessential, small-town holiday celebration."

"Your plan worked." The only way the day could've been better was if he'd finally given her a kiss.

"I'm glad…" As if reading her mind, he leaned closer, only Mackenzie blocked his way. "And right about now, I'm really wishing my mom felt good enough for us to use her as a sitter."

BY THE TIME THE FIREWORKS started, Tristan felt a little guilty that he was happy Mackenzie had finally been fed and fallen asleep in her carrier. But just a little.

Brynn rested her head on his shoulders as they stared up at the show. "The perfect end to the perfect day."

"Not quite." Rolling over, partially blocking her view, he said, "Pretty sure I've wanted to do this from the first day I saw you." He hovered over her for what felt like forever, drinking her in. Kaleidoscopic light from the fireworks transformed Brynn into an exotic creature from a lovely dream. He'd waited so long to kiss her, instinctively knowing she'd taste so good, that he took his time completing that last inch. When finally his lips touched hers, the sensation was so intense, he wasn't sure he could handle keeping things G-rated.

Her soft groan only encouraged him into deepening his exploration with a sweep of his tongue.

The fireworks exploding over their heads had nothing on the beautiful release of having wondered so long what this moment might be like only to finally, happily know.

"Now we have perfection," he finally said, framing her face with his hands.

Fingers in his hair, she nodded before drawing him in for more.

IT TOOK THIRTY MINUTES TO WIND their way through the traffic leaving the lake, but Brynn hadn't minded. Both kids were asleep in the back of her SUV and Tristan was at the wheel. In the dash light's glow, he looked so impossibly handsome she had to pinch herself to believe he was even temporarily hers. Being with him was not only a dangerous game for her heart, but Cayden's. Though she wasn't yet convinced she and Tristan were in this for the long haul, she feared her son already was.

"What're you thinking about?" Tristan asked.

Taking her time formulating just the right answer, she said, "Pretty much the same issues we've already been over a hundred times."

He eased his fingers between hers. "My leaving?"

She nodded.

"Would it help if I told you I'm worried, too?"

"You mean like you're considering asking for a discharge?"

"I wouldn't go that far. The navy's my life. But I'm worried about Mom and leaving Cayden. Hell, maybe I should ask my CO for more time?"

His speech touched his life's every concern but her. Oh, she didn't doubt for a moment he was attracted to her, but obviously he didn't share the deep affection for her he did for her son. She would never expect him to care for her like he did his mother, but still, it might be nice to occupy some small space in his heart.

"When are you and Cayden headed to St. Louis for Mack's game?"

"Last weekend of this month. The team's making our flight arrangements and pretty much handling everything else."

"That's exciting." He gave her hand a squeeze.

More like terrifying. At the lowest point she'd ever been in her life, her so-called friends and thousands more she'd never even personally met had shown her the proverbial door. They'd transferred their hatred for Mack and what they'd believed he'd done to the game onto her and her innocent son. Via internet, she'd kept up with St. Louis current events and learned since the Cardinals punished the players and members of team management who'd really been involved with the cheating scandal that the public knew Mack's name to be cleared.

"Not really."

"Why?"

"Can you believe the team has forwarded letters to me from fans? Apologizing for believing Mack had done anything wrong? I've read a few, but put the rest in the attic in case Cayden one day wants to see." As long as she lived, she'd never forget the pain and shame that seemed to have taken up permanent residence in her heart. "I'm glad everyone's back to their hero worship of Mack, but is it wrong for me to want my own apologies?" Especially from the husband she'd implicitly trusted? Checking to make sure Cayden was still soundly asleep, she said, "Sometimes late at night, I find myself hating Mack for what he did to our lives. I get that his intentions were noble, but it went so wrong.

Didn't I deserve to at the very least be involved in his decision to go forward with such an asinine plan?"

Still holding her hand, Tristan lifted it to his mouth, kissing her palm. "For what it's worth, I'm sorry. I'd give anything to be able to erase your pain."

"Thanks." Staring out the window at the darkness beyond, she asked, "Want to tag along?"

"To Mack's big game?"

Throat aching with tears she refused to spill, she nodded. "I'm not sure I can do it alone."

Pulling into her drive, he said, "I'd be honored. Who knows? It might even turn out to be fun."

"This is a nice surprise." Back to work after the long weekend, Brynn turned off the hose she'd been using to water the nursery's annuals to give Donna and Georgia hugs. "I take it you're feeling much better?"

"Still moving slower than I'd like," Donna said, "but the doc says I need exercise, and since Georgia was already headed this way, I figured what would it hurt to tag along?"

"Plus," Georgia interjected, "we'd both like the details of your Independence Day date."

Recalling Tristan's kiss raised heat in Brynn's cheeks.

"That good, huh?" Georgia winked before fanning herself.

"You're awful," Brynn said of her friend. "We had a great time. End of story."

"Uh-huh…" Donna pretended to study yellow marigolds. "Which is why Tristan's going with you to St. Louis at the end of the month?"

"Strictly for moral support—and of course, to heft luggage."

Georgia laughed. "That's my girl."

"Seriously, though," Donna said, "you do like him, right?"

On that note, Brynn resumed watering. "It's not as if Tristan and I are in junior high. Of course, I *like* him, but our lives are more complicated."

"Well, sure, but—"

"Where's that baby?" Was that Georgia's thinly veiled attempt to change the subject?

"She's inside, napping. I have her monitor." Brynn tapped the plastic receiver affixed to the waistband of her jeans.

"Such a wonderful invention," Georgia mused.

"Don't think I can't see what you two are doing." Donna deadheaded a flower with enough vehemence to give Brynn cause for concern. "My whole heart episode has me realizing I'm not getting younger. I need to know Tristan's in good hands, and Brynn, I like you."

Brynn set down her spray nozzle to take Donna's hands. "Thank you, but by your own admission, you're doing better and Tristan's not exactly proposing to me. Even if he were, I wouldn't accept. We hardly know each other."

"But you're getting there, right?"

Brynn shook her head…

When her children were grown, would she have Donna's clarity? The certainty that her child was on the right path? From reading Donna's postsurgical material, Brynn knew oftentimes patients grew depressed, but Brynn couldn't be held responsible for Tristan's mother's happiness. She was having a tough enough time finding her own.

Chapter Fourteen

A sold-out crowd had shown up to Mack's game at Busch Stadium. Or maybe just to see the spectacle of his children and widow paraded onto the pitcher's mound. Forty-six thousand people.

"Mom," Cayden said moments before the ceremony began, reaching for her hand, "I'm scared."

"It's okay," she assured, holding Mackenzie a little closer. "This'll all be over soon."

"Welcome," the commissioner said into his microphone, "thank you all for joining us on this special afternoon." He paused a moment while fans cheered. "Today, we celebrate the life of our fallen hero, second baseman, Mack Langtoine."

As the standing crowd roared, Brynn began to tremble. It started from deep inside and threatened to manifest in tears. Struggling to maintain her dignity, she tuned out the rest of the commissioner's speech, focusing instead on Tristan. Located far above her in the owner's suite, though she couldn't see him, she felt him, imagined him on the field with her, his arms securely around not only her, but Cayden and Mackenzie.

The commissioner continued, "In the past year, this organization has suffered. As have you—our valued fans. I want to assure you all matters of impropriety have been addressed and as this team draws nearer to play-offs, it's time for healing. For a rebirth of the spirit of goodwill and sportsmanship that help make this game the greatest in the world!"

The crowd exploded with cheers and applaud.

The sun's heat—the deafening sound—was too much. Still, Brynn stood her ground. These people who threw eggs at her family's home were now welcoming her back with open arms.

After the mayor gave Cayden the key to the city in his father's honor, the team owner announced the retirement of Mack's jersey. The minister of the church she and Mack had attended led the stadium in prayer.

Cayden tossed the ceremonial first pitch, then they were whisked from the field and up into the owner's suite. The whole thing had taken maybe fifteen minutes, but it felt as though they were reliving the past year all over again. She knew everyone meant well, and many of Mack's closest friends on the team—including the team manager—told her from the start they'd never believed Mack had done wrong.

Cayden had again taken hold of her hand, at least until spotting Tristan. He then ran to him for a hug.

"Hey," Tristan said, shielding them from the suite's other guests, "how are you? Was it as hard as you thought?"

She nodded, fearing if she spoke, she wouldn't be able to hold back the tears. "C-can you please get us out of here?"

As if computing the most efficient escape route, he looked around, then, hand on the small of her back, propelled her and her children from the stadium.

LESS THAN AN HOUR LATER, Tristan had transported Brynn a world away to the museum at the foot of the St. Louis Arch. While Cayden played with interactive history displays, Tristan pushed Mackenzie's stroller with one hand and with his other, held Brynn loosely around her waist. "Better?"

She nodded, resting her head against his strong shoulder. Exhaustion clung to her as if she'd just emerged from battle. "I'm bone-deep tired. This how you feel after finishing one of your missions?"

"Used to." He steered them around a covered wagon display. "I've done so many, they've become routine."

"I wouldn't want to ever go through something like this enough times for it to feel normal."

"Don't blame you." He kissed the top of her head. "But know what?"

"What?"

"You looked sexy out there, with that cute sundress swaying around your legs."

"Tristan!" She landed a playful swat to his chest. "I'm being serious."

"Me, too." He winked, snagging her by her waist again to draw her in for the sweetest of kisses. It was the kind of kiss that weakened her knees and coaxed butterflies to flight in her belly. The kind of kiss that restored not only her faith in humanity, but her own future.

ON THE FLIGHT FROM ST. LOUIS to Dallas, Tristan envied Brynn's, Cayden's and even Mackenzie's ability to sleep.

Typically, he could drift off anywhere, be it in the belly of a C-130 or submarine. Though his body felt plenty tired, his brain refused to shut down.

The weekend brought him closer than ever to Brynn and her kids. It also served as a reminder that he'd already had a family and lost it. What if the same thing happened again? What if he made the ultimate play for Brynn, asking her to marry him, only to have her eventually leave just like Andrea and Jack?

Brynn stirred, shifting to rest her head on his shoulder.

He liked being there for not only her, but Cayden and Mackenzie. They gave him reason to be strong. When his mom was in the hospital, he'd been so afraid she wouldn't make it. Having already lost his dad, he couldn't imagine losing her, too. The only thing helping him through was knowing no matter what, he'd still have Brynn and her crew by his side. But considering his career, did he even have the right to ask them to stay with him?

"Sir?" a flight attendant asked. "Can I get any of you a soft drink?"

"No, thanks."

She smiled, already moving on to the row behind him.

While he hadn't wanted a beverage, he appreciated her question from the standpoint that at least it had interrupted his twisted chain of thought.

He had to once and for all get Andrea's poison from his system. Lots of SEALs had amazing home lives. Look at his friends Deacon and Garrett. Tristan being a SEAL didn't make him a bad guy to be with, but better. No one could watch over this trio like him.

True, his conscience pointed out, but he'd once believed the same about Andrea and Jack and they no longer wanted his brand of protection.

"ABOUT TIME YOU ALL GOT HOME." Despite a steady downpour, Donna's smile was bright. "I missed you."

"We missed you, too." For Brynn, entering the place where Tristan had grown up, with its hodgepodge of furnishings and walls hung with homemade art, surprisingly did feel like home. With Mack's game behind her, and the St. Louis house sold, she felt renewed, as if anything was possible—including maybe Donna's dream of Brynn being with her son. The one issue she couldn't seem to reconcile was the fact that even if she and Tristan did end up together on a permanent basis, would she be any more capable of accepting his job than Andrea? Only not because he was gone a lot of the time—that, she understood. What she feared she couldn't handle was his being in constant danger. She'd already had one man she loved shot. Not that she was anywhere near loving Tristan, but his kisses had left her in an awful lot of *like*.

"Miss Donna?" Cayden crossed his legs. "May I please use your bathroom?"

"You certainly may. It's just down the hall." She pointed, and he ran that direction.

"Your color's better." Tristan kissed his mom's cheek.

"I'm feeling better every day. In fact, Brynn, if you don't mind, could you take me to garden club Saturday?"

"I'd love to."

"Thanks." Straightening in her armchair, she tossed off the crocheted throw she'd had on her lap. "Now bring me that baby."

Watching Tristan's mom play with Mackenzie, talking to her in a silly, sing-song voice while the baby alternately cooed and grabbed for her reading glasses, filled Brynn with deep satisfaction. It'd been a while since she'd had a mother figure in her life, and the more she was around Donna, the more Brynn enjoyed her company.

"Whew." Cayden was back. "Thanks a lot, Miss Donna. I thought I was gonna die."

"Well, we can't have that," Tristan's mom teased. "Do you like muffins?"

"Yeah," he said with an eager nod. "Got some?"

"Cayden," Brynn scolded.

"What?" he asked, "I figured she wouldn't talk about 'em if she didn't have any. Unless you want us to go buy you some?"

She laughed. "Thank you, honey, but I just made a batch. They're cooling on the counter. Go right through that door to the kitchen and have one."

"Can I have two?"

"Cayden!" Brynn thought she'd taught her son better. Apparently, they needed to revisit Manners 101.

"It's okay." Donna passed the baby to Tristan, then pushed up from the chair. "You can have as many as you want. Come on." She held out his hand to him. "They're made with bran, so I'm going to have one, too."

"It's nice seeing her with him," Tristan said once they'd left the room. "She misses Jack as much as I do. She's a wonderful grandmother."

"It shows." Just one more reason Brynn grew fonder of Tristan every day—his dear mom.

"ALL RIGHT GUYS," COACH Jason said to the Mud Bugs before the last game of the tournament that determined bragging rights for the best little league team in the county. Even for late August, the day was especially steamy and hot. "This is it. If you win today, we'll move on to the state tourney in New Orleans. How cool is that?"

The team cheered.

Tristan watched the remainder of his friend's pep talk

to the boys from the edge of the field. He had mixed
feelings about the game. Of course, he wanted the Mud
Bugs to win, but he'd already told his CO he planned on
returning to base by September 1. Tuning out Jason, he
looked to the crowded stands. Parents and grandparents
and friends of both teams filled the regional ballpark's
stands. Out of everyone present, though, Tristan only
had eyes for Brynn.

She'd worn the special Mud Bug T-shirt Jason's wife
had made—there was even a tiny one especially for
Mackenzie. Both of his girls rocked their white sun hats
and jean shorts. Somehow, over the course of the summer, they'd become *his*. He thought of them and Cayden
morning, noon and night. He was returning to work not
only because he needed the money, but clarity. Maybe
time spent away from them would help him ultimately
decide if another marriage was right for him.

Brynn didn't like talking about his leaving any more
than he did. And so for the past few weeks, they'd played
as if he'd be in Ruin Bayou forever. They'd shared family meals and private kisses and more than anything, he
wished they could just go on like this forever. Unfortunately, there wasn't a lot of call for his line of work in
northern Louisiana.

"On three," Jason said, "all hands in for Mug Bugs!"

After a countdown, the team stacked hands and
shouted, "Mud Bugs!"

Despite the heat, the teams played hard.

By the fourth inning, the Mud Bugs and Comets were
tied at five. There were already two outs by the time
Cayden made it to bat. Tension balled in Tristan's stomach. At this point in the season, he was pretty sure he
wanted Cayden to succeed as badly as the boy wanted
it for himself.

"Come on, Cayden!" Brynn shouted from the stands.

"Hit it hard!" Donna shouted, with Georgia chiming in.

"Slam it home, Cay!" Vivian called with Mackenzie hitching a ride on her lap.

Tristan's pulse was on a runaway course.

With a teammate on third and another on second, Cayden's expression was one of steely determination. Lips pressed tight, eyes on the pitcher, his stance and hold on the bat were perfection.

"Come on, bud," Tristan said under his breath. "All you've gotta do is swing your little heart out…"

"Strike one!" the ump called.

You can do it…

"Strike two!"

Come on, Cayden. Do it for your dad. Do it for me.

The pitcher wound up and threw a flawless right curve. Countless times Tristan and Cayden had practiced for just this scenario, and now, during the most crucial game of his little league career, Cayden put all that hard work to use by hitting the most amazingly gorgeous home run Tristan had ever seen.

"Yeah!" Tristan shouted as Cayden dashed for first base. "Run, Cayden, run!"

Brynn was laughing and crying.

Georgia, Donna and Vivian, along with every other Mud Bug fan, went nuts cheering for their team.

Now that they'd taken a three-point lead, as long as they played their cards right, it was a pretty good bet victory was near. But honestly, even if they lost, Tristan's world shone a lot brighter.

When Cayden had run all the bases to home, Jason got to him first, slapping him a well-deserved high five. After his excited teammates had also congratulated him,

Tristan lifted him off the ground in a giant bear hug. "You're amazing! That was the best hit ever!"

"As good as my dad's?" Cayden asked.

"Absolutely. Your dad would be so proud."

"Did Mom see?"

"Did she see?" Tristan laughed. "Bud, look up in the stands, she still hasn't stopped crying. She's so happy for you. You're the star of the game."

"Really?" He looked to the stands in time to catch her wave.

Vivian held up Mackenzie's little hands to cheer.

"Look at Mac!" He pointed at his baby sister. "She's funny!" If there was anything that could top a home run in Tristan's eyes, it was seeing Cayden actually smile and wave back at the baby he'd once so greatly resented.

To CELEBRATE THEIR WIN—AFTER Cayden's big hit, the Comets fizzled—the Mud Bugs partied at Coach Jason's. His wife, Trina, had run home after the game to start the grill and by the time all the other parents added side dishes, a karaoke machine and plenty of water toys for the pool, a wonderful time was being had by all.

Brynn sat on the pool steps, helping Mackenzie dip her toes in the warm water. After being too rowdy for the little kids, the boys had been banished to the deep end. "This feels heavenly."

"No kidding." Tristan knelt so the water reached his neck. "A couple of times in the outfield today, I wasn't sure I'd make it."

"What?" She feigned shock. "A big, strong guy like you bothered by a little heat?"

He splashed in her direction, but not hard enough for Mackenzie to get wet. "While you were up in the stands, chowing on three snow cones—I counted—me and the guys were out there hard at work."

"You counted?" Now she splashed him.

"What can I say? I *really* wanted one."

"We'll get you one tomorrow—make a day of it. Take Cayden minigolfing. After all the work he's done this summer, he deserves multiple celebrations. You, too, for that matter. His hit today wouldn't have been possible without you."

He ducked his gaze. "He'd have eventually gotten better. Just would've taken more time."

"Don't discount what you did for him. He's changed so much, and all for the better. All because of you. His therapist even says you're good for him."

"Brynn…" Not meeting her gaze, he swished his hands through the lukewarm water.

"What? Go ahead, take credit where credit's due. I'm not sure what Cayden would do without you. You've been so great for him—and me."

When he finally got around to replying, he still looked everywhere but to her. "I appreciate your kind words. Really, I do, but…"

"Wait—is this weird mood of yours about you leaving?"

"Yes. We've talked about this, remember?"

Stomach churning more from his gloomy expression than too much potato salad, she said, "Sure. We talked about it, but I didn't think anything was definitively decided."

"Of course it was. For a while. You've just been sticking your head in the sand." His words were uncharacteristically cruel.

"Where is this coming from? Especially on what's supposed to be a happy occasion."

He stood, walking the short distance to sit beside her. "Look, I'm sorry. I wasn't going to say anything about it, but when you assumed I was available to play tomorrow, I—"

"What are you doing?" she asked with a heavy heart and narrowed eyes.

"Packing for my trek back to base."

Chapter Fifteen

"You're kidding?" Brynn's tear-filled gaze pierced Tristan as painfully as if one of the boys had rammed a marshmallow-roasting stick through his heart.

"I have to go. You know that."

"No." She vehemently shook her head. "You haven't talked about it in so long, I thought that meant you'd changed your mind. That you'd decided to stay here, with me and Cayden and Mac."

"Let's not do this here." He rose from the pool.

"Then where?" Mackenzie on her hip, she followed him across the wood decking. "Tristan Bartoni, don't you dare drop a bombshell like this one on me and then walk away."

"Ask Vivian to watch the kids," he said in a low tone. "Then meet me in the truck."

With him still in swim trucks, drenched with sweat in the front seat of his ride, he watched Brynn emerge from the house, tossing Vivian her keys. She expected their talk to take so long that her friend would need to drive home with the baby?

"All right," she said upon climbing into the truck beside him, "I've got all the time we need."

In heavy silence, he drove to Turtle Lake. Though it was technically a city park, due to vandalism, aside from holidays the gate was usually kept locked. Jason once told him there was a spare key to the gate's chained padlock housed in a magnetic holder behind the main sign.

He parked the truck and got out.

The key was where he'd expected. He pulled the truck through, closing the gate behind them.

Parked in the lot, he turned off the truck's engine, then sat, waiting for Brynn to talk first.

His wait wasn't long. "You are some piece of work."

"How so?"

"You told me you hadn't decided whether or not you're leaving, but all along you knew."

"No." He hated fighting with her, especially when they were left with so little time. "That's not how it was. And if you don't mind, it's hot as hell in here. Let's head down to the lake."

"Whatever."

He gestured for her to lead the way down the dirt trail. "I don't understand how you can be upset with me for needing to work."

"I'm not. What I'm frustrated about is that I thought this was a decision we were making together. I—" At the lake's edge, she spun to face him. "I thought you felt the same as me, that we should take it slow, but one day, we might share a future?"

"I want that, too, but all of this is happening too soon."

"Is it really, Tristan? Or are you just too scared to even consider another commitment?"

"Of course I'm scared," he shouted, startling a flock of crows. "Aren't you? Hell, Mack's only been gone a year. What do you even want with me?"

"Are you kidding?" She lifted her hand as if angry

enough to hit him, but then stormed down the shore. "I loved Mack with every breath of my being, but he made some horrible judgment calls that turned out not only to kill him, but a large part of *me*. Being with you makes me feel normal—like I might actually have a shot at living again, after all. But now?" After a brittle laugh, she raised her arms only to slap them to her sides. "I hate you. I seriously, honest to God hate you."

"No, you don't." He went to her, cupping her precious face. She could say anything to him, but not that. *Anything*, but that.

"I...hate...you!" she said between sobs.

"No..." He kissed her hard, forcing her tears and angry words away. When she kissed him with equal fervor, he backed her against a picnic table, hiking up her bikini cover.

Lips still pressed to hers, he dragged down her bikini bottoms. She helped by wriggling her legs.

He tugged at his swim trunks until he freed his erection. "You sure this is what you want?"

Kissing his neck and chest, she nodded.

Assuming it'd been a while, he explored her first with his fingers. When she cried out in pleasure with her fingers in his hair, he entered her—slowly at first, but then lifting her, urging her legs around his midsection while pumping increasingly deeper and harder.

Their kissing turned frenzied.

Late-afternoon sun baked already sweat-slick bodies.

Only when she cried out again, stiffening in his arms for an instant before total release, did he give in to his own happy ending.

Arms around his neck, his member still inside her, she said in a voice raspy with passion, "I'm sorry we fought."

"Me, too."

Still holding her, he stepped all the way out of his trunks, backing their fevered bodies into the lake's cool water.

When she kissed him again, moaning her pleasure, he feared never being able to let her go. She'd bewitched him, and he'd become her all-too-willing captive.

AFTER THEIR SWIM, WHILE BRYNN shyly dressed, Tristan found the picnic blanket they'd used for the Fourth stashed in the back of his truck. He stretched it beneath the tree where they'd first kissed, and they napped for a good hour.

Brynn woke before him, taking a mental picture she'd forever carry. Now that they'd made love, had everything changed? She knew he had to return to Virginia Beach, but would it be only temporarily? What they'd shared had said more than words ever could. His body made promises he wouldn't dare break. There was no way the two of them could share something so intense without it carrying significant meaning, right?

He woke to catch her staring. "Like what you see?"

"Seriously? That's the first thing you say to me?"

He pulled her against him, kissing her until her bikini top was too much fabric between her breasts and his rock-solid chest. "Better?" he asked with a dead-sexy grin.

"Getting there..."

When he next kissed her, she nipped his lower lip.

"Ouch. I never pegged you for the type who liked it rough."

"I'm not. But sometimes a bad boy like you needs punishing..."

He laughed, rolling atop her for kissing and exploring and making love at a much more leisurely pace.

An hour later, back in the lake as the sun made a lazy fall from the sky, she said, "I never thought to ask, but are there alligators in this water?"

"Probably." He kissed the tip of her nose. "Also, a few water moccasins, snapping turtles and maybe even alligator gar."

"So we're swimming why?"

He tossed back his head and laughed. "Damn good question."

Lifting her into his arms, he carried her from the water, kissing her along the way. He set her on the picnic table before asking, "Want me to build a fire or should we check on the kids?"

Hugging him, she said, "I like the sound of that—the two of us together, checking on *our* kids. Because you know Cayden already loves you like a father."

He bowed his handsome head. "I love him, too."

"Since you're not leaving, are we back on for tomorrow? We'll already be in Shreveport, so I thought we might also hit that new Bossier City walking mall by the river. Maybe see a movie? Vivian said the theater's really nice. Plus, Bass Pro's always fun."

"Whoa." Holding up his hands, he slowly backed away. "I think we have a misunderstanding. Brynn, being with you just now was amazing—beyond amazing—but that's all it can be. I can't commit. Not right now. You know that. I'm a mess inside and afraid. As much as I enjoyed what just happened, that doesn't change the fact that first thing Monday morning, I'm leaving."

"HE'S HORRIBLE," VIVIAN SAID when Brynn finished telling her the shameful outcome of her afternoon with

Tristan. After more bitter fighting and tears, she'd had him drop her at her friend's house so she'd have her kids and car. "I don't know why I encouraged you to go for him. Obviously, it was a bad call."

Temporarily out of tears, Brynn sniffled.

"Know what?" Vivian moved to the sofa, patting Brynn's leg. "This is probably for the best. Sean said they just hired a new guy at his firm, and he's single. Do you know how rare it is to find a single attorney our age? I'll have Sean get his number and we'll have a barbecue."

"Stop," Brynn said. "Last thing I need is to meet another man. I was stupid for ever letting myself fall for Tristan. I knew better from the start, but he was so good with Cayden and easy to talk to and always making me laugh—he even mows the lawn."

Vivian chimed in, "Lord, does he look fine doing that…"

"See? That's what I'm talking about. He was too good to be true and I was too blind to see."

"What are you going to tell Cayden? He'll be crushed when Tristan leaves."

Groaning, Brynn leaned forward, covering her face with her hands. "I don't know. I don't know."

"He was so happy after today's game."

After losing his second *father* in a little over a year, Brynn feared her son might never be happy again.

"YOU'VE MADE A LOT OF BAD decisions over the years," Tristan's mother said Sunday morning while he changed the oil in his truck, "but this one takes the cake, cookies and muffins."

"Thanks, Mom. Appreciate the vote of confidence."

She snorted. "Pardon my French, but if you ask me, you're a damn fool."

"Didn't ask anyone—let alone, you." On his back, he tugged extra hard on the nut holding the oil pan in place and damn near got a face full of dirty, black goo.

"I heard you call her earlier about setting up a time to say your goodbyes to little Cayden. I never took you to be deliberately cruel."

"What's that supposed to mean?" He finished draining the old oil. "I did everything in my power to help the kid."

"Agreed—including forging a genuine relationship. He believes you care for him."

"I do."

"Then how can you stand to leave him? Over the summer, I've seen the two of you together. He worships you, and it's plain to see whenever you're around him that to you, he's become like a second son."

"Please, Mom…" Tristan reassembled the oil pan, then slid out from under the truck. "Just like I do with Jack, I'll keep in touch. I'll see him every time I come see you."

"Wouldn't it be easier to just marry his mom?"

"Then what?" He hated snapping at his mother but wasn't sure how else to get his point across. "How am I supposed to support a family with no job? Should I move back here and clerk at a convenience store? I'm a SEAL. That's all I know how to be. Why tie down Brynn and her kids to a man who not only regularly gets shot at, but is never even home?"

She turned her back on him to huff onto the front porch. "Excuses, excuses."

"It's reality!" he shouted, kicking his truck's front tire.

She'd already slammed the door.

"Why're you crying, Mom?"

The Sunday afternoon sun cast a lacy shadow through the curtains and onto the hardwood floor. Brynn squinted and dried her eyes with the pillowcase before rolling in the bed to face her son. When she'd put Mackenzie down for her nap, she assumed she'd been alone. "Cayden. Thought you and Dom were in your fort?"

"We were, but he had to leave to go school shopping." He sat on the foot of the bed. "When're we gonna go?"

"Real soon, sweetie."

"Okay."

She sat up, blowing her nose on a tissue she took from the box on the nightstand.

"You never did say why you were crying. You sick?"

Sort of. Did she prep him? Telling him why Tristan would be over in a little under thirty minutes?

"'Cause if you are, I can get you medicine. I promised Tristan I'd take care of you and he told me a SEAL never goes back on his word."

Really? But then Tristan had never made her promises as much as she'd made assumptions.

"Thanks, pumpkin, but I don't need anything but a nice, big hug."

"Okay!" He bounced over the bed to ambush her from behind.

From downstairs came the sound of the doorbell.

"Who's here?" he asked, jumping his way off the bed.

Brynn's stomach knotted.

It was the wrong time of year for Girl Scout cookies and Georgia was spending the afternoon with her granddaughter's family, which could only mean Tristan was early.

Cayden bounded down the stairs. "It's Tristan! I'm letting him in, Mom!"

"Hey, bud." Brynn heard Tristan say from where she hovered at the top of the stairs. She couldn't imagine Cayden's reaction—didn't want to.

"Mom!" her son shouted. "Tristan's here!"

Her flighty hands trying to bring order to her hair, she took her time on the stairs. Should she act surprised he was here? Would he have wanted her to get Cayden prepared for his visit? On the flip side, why would she help him break her son's heart?

Upon seeing him sitting ramrod straight on the sofa, holding a faded ball cap in his hands, all her dry mouth could handle was a simple, "Hi."

They shared a long, cold look.

Her body stupidly craved his touch. She hated that— how her brain knew he was trouble, but the rest of her only wanted more.

"Wanna play catch?" Cayden asked. "I left my mitt at Dom's, but I can ride my bike real fast to get it."

Tristan cleared his throat, looking to Brynn as if she might better know how to deliver his news. But he'd be wrong. "That sounds fun," he finally said, "but I need you to sit down." He patted the sofa cushion beside him. "I've got something kind of important to run by you."

"Okay. Then we can go outside?"

"Nope. Not today." Tristan repeatedly flipped the cap. A nervous reaction? Buying time to think up something to say? Or all of the above?

"How come?" Cayden asked with a scowl. "Now that I made a home run, I've gotta get ready for the state tourney."

"I know, and Coach Jason already promised me he'd find someone to help."

Cayden cocked his head. "How come you can't keep doing it?"

"Remember how we talked about me being in the navy?"

"Uh-huh…"

Tristan forced a deep breath. "Well, when my son, Jack, moved to California, I was kinda upset. But now that I feel better, I have to get back to work."

"Okay…" Cayden still looked confused. "But you're gonna get a job like Mom, right? Where you just go away during the day and then you're home when I get out of school or practice?"

"Not exactly."

Cayden yawned, which Brynn took as a sign that he hadn't anywhere near grasped what Tristan was saying. "Then you're just gonna be gone sometimes like my dad? But then you'll be home?"

Handing him the hat, Tristan said, "I want you to have this. It was mine when I used to be a Mud Bug with your dad."

"Really?" His eyes widened. "That's cool. But why don't you give it to Jack?"

"He likes surfing and skateboarding more than baseball. And anyway, this hat means a lot to me, and so… so do you." Tristan's voice cracked. "When you wear it, I want you to do me a favor and think about me, okay?"

"Sure. I guess…" Cayden put Tristan's childhood hat backward on his head. It was a perfect fit. "But whenever you're here, I think about you all the time."

"That's just it." Noticeably pale, Tristan looked to Brynn, but she looked away. He forged ahead. "I'm going to be living in a place called Virginia Beach, and it's kind of a long way away."

"Wait—" Cayden's eyes filled with tears. "You mean

you're moving? Like me and Mom did when we left St. Louis? So like I've never seen any of my friends or teachers or my dad ever again, that's gonna be the same as you?"

"Bud…" To his credit, Tristan's eyes had grown equally red.

"W-why are you doing this?" Cayden asked on a coughing sob. "I thought you loved me and Mom and Mackenzie? B-but if you do love us, then you wouldn't leave."

"Your dad left, and he loved you."

"That isn't the same!" Cayden jumped to his feet. "My doctor says bad guys killed my dad! He's dead! You're just leaving because you don't like us anymore!"

"Ah, Cayden, that's not how it is at all…"

"I hate you!" Brynn's boy shouted on his way out the door. "I hate you and you can keep your stupid hat!" Cayden pitched it at him. "I don't ever want to think of you again!"

"Swell." Hands tucked in his jean pockets, Tristan said, "Like mother, like son."

Chapter Sixteen

Cayden ran and ran through the neighborhood until he was kind of lost. But then he saw Miss Georgia pulling weeds out of her backyard and he remembered how nice she'd always been to him, so he went to ask her for help.

"Hello, there." She smiled when he came close. "You're a fine mess. All sweaty. Want some of my special pink lemonade?"

"Yes, ma'am."

She pointed to the pretty covered swing she sat on a lot when she looked at her flowers. "Sit a spell and I'll be right back." Over her shoulder, she asked, "Want cookies, too?"

He nodded.

By the time she got back, carrying a big plate of chocolate chip cookies and a plastic cup with lemonade and lots of ice, he'd stopped crying, but didn't feel better.

While he ate cookies, Miss Georgia sat next to him, making the swing sway just a little with her bare feet. "Now that you've had refreshment, how about telling me what's got you in a dither?"

He looked at her all squinty. "I'm not really sure what that means."

"It's just a fancy way of asking what has you upset."

"Lots." After drinking half his lemonade, he let out a big breath. "Guess what Tristan just told me?"

"What?" She leaned in closer.

"He's leaving Ruin Bayou and never coming back."

"Really…" She didn't seem as surprised as he'd been. "I was afraid of that."

He grabbed a cookie from the plate she held on her lap. "How'd you even know?"

"I'm *very* old, so not much surprises me." She put her arm around his shoulders and gave him a squeeze. "Things do make me sad, though. And this is for sure one of those things. I'd have bet good money Tristan was going to make you a great second dad."

Cayden tried hard not to, but he started crying again. "M-me, too."

"I'LL BE DAMNED…" Tristan's old roomie, fellow SEAL Calder Remington, held open the apartment door. "We were all beginning to wonder if we'd ever see you again."

Tristan shrugged on his way through the door. "Thanks for letting me in. Not sure what I did with my key."

"You look like hammered shit."

"You're too kind." Dropping his duffel bag on the living-room floor, Tristan added, "Feel like it, too."

"Everyone else know you're back?"

"Just the CO."

Exhausted from the eighteen-hour drive, Tristan fell into a recliner. The place smelled the same—like beer and stale pizza. The upstairs neighbor's base still thumped through the ceiling and there were still no knickknacks to speak of or pictures hung on the walls. He used to feel comfortable here. Now it felt lifeless and sterile. He much preferred Brynn's or even his mom's. But it was too late to second-guess his decision to leave now.

He hadn't even given Brynn a proper hug goodbye—let alone the final kiss he'd craved.

"Then you know?"

Tristan had closed his eyes, imagining her gorgeous freckled face, but he opened one eye to look at his old friend. "Know what?"

"We're shipping out in the morning. Somalia. Should be a *real* good time."

HAVING SPENT LABOR DAY WITH Vivian and Sean, Brynn worked hard on Tuesday keeping herself busy getting Cayden ready for school.

Since his last talk with Tristan, her son hadn't been the same. He clung to her like he hadn't since immediately following Mack's death and seeing his smile had become as elusive as spotting a rainbow-striped unicorn in the backyard.

He was watching a favorite Disney movie when the phone rang.

The caller ID number was so odd she almost didn't answer. "Hello?" she asked out of boredom.

"Brynn?" Her racing heart recognized the voice before her head.

"Tristan?" Why was he calling? They'd already said more than she could bear.

"Please don't hang up. I'm calling from Germany and I don't have long before catching my next ride."

Questions raced through her mind. What was he doing so far away? Was he on a mission? Was it dangerous?

"Listen, I don't know when I'll be back in the country, but before I leave, I have to tell you again I'm sorry."

Tears welled in her eyes and knotted her throat.

"I don't regret leaving—well, I do, but for selfish reasons. I want better for you than me. I want you to have a real, stay-home kind of husband and for Cayden to have a dad who's there for every ball game."

"Oh—" A ragged laugh escaped the lump in her throat. "So you think I can just head out on a street corner to replace you? Maybe put an ad in the paper?"

"Dammit, Brynn, you know what I mean."

"No, Tristan, I don't know anything about you. I thought I did, but then you made love to me and left town. Wham bam, thank you, ma'am."

"It wasn't like that and you know it."

She sighed, turning her back to the living room in case seven-year-old ears listened. "Then tell me what it was like, because I'm kind of confused."

"I called to hopefully give us both closure, but I can see that's not happening."

"You want closure?" she snapped. "You got it. Never call me again."

"Brynn… Come on, don't be like this. I don't know when we'll talk again."

"Then you shouldn't have left." So furious she was shaking, Brynn hung up the phone.

One second later, she regretted it and frantically tried calling back, but she got a recording about the number being only for outgoing calls.

"Mom?" Cayden joined her in the kitchen. "Who was on the phone? You sounded mad."

"No, sweetie." She comforted herself by giving him a hug. "Just someone trying to sell something I wasn't in the mood to buy."

TRISTAN'S SUPPOSEDLY in-and-out mission to Somalia turned into what was starting to feel like a never-ending siege. A particularly violent drug cartel had attempted a government takeover and his team had been charged with tracking the lovely bunch of thugs. Tristan and his buddies were posing as an oil exploration crew while gathering intelligence. Months had passed during which he hadn't been able to get word to Jack or Cayden, let alone his mom or Brynn.

Tristan had a couple of great pics of Jack he kept in his chest pocket, along with a print he'd made before leaving the States of the Fourth of July shot he'd taken of the Langtoine clan. As it was early November, meaning they were fortunate enough to be enjoying the Somalian *Dayr,* or fall rainy season, everything he owned was damp. He kept his pics in a Ziploc baggy, insuring his most valuable possessions remained safe and dry.

"Look at that much more, you're going to burn a hole in it."

"With my laser eyes?" Tristan shot Garrett a look he hoped conveyed to his longtime friend to mind his own business.

"You don't have to be testy. It's not like most of us haven't been in your place at one time or another. I miss Eve and our kids so bad it hurts, but we just gotta soldier through."

Tristan turned off his flashlight and sighed. "Yeah, well, what if I told you I'm tired?"

"Aren't we all? But this is what we signed up for."

"I know, but maybe it's not worth it."

Resting on his side, Garrett bunched the T-shirt he used as a pillow under his head. "You mean being a SEAL?"

"Yeah. You ever think of hanging up your Trident?"

"Hell, no. Eve knows what my being a SEAL means and is okay with it. We both lead full lives and when we come together, it's still great—like a do-over honeymoon."

"TMI," Tristan said with a grunt. "Problem is, my lady—or at least the woman I'd like to be mine—says she'd be okay with me leaving, but Andrea once said the same. Look how swell that turned out. But, hell, I can't stand being away from her or her kids. Or Jack. My head's constantly spinning, trying to figure out a way I don't have to give up everything I've ever known to get the one thing I now want."

"I ALMOST HATE TO ASK," Donna said over Christmas dinner, "but have you heard from Tristan since his last call?"

Brynn shook her head, hoping Cayden and his big ears hadn't overheard. Any mention of Tristan upset him to the point Brynn had pretty much banished his name. She wasn't sure if this was handling Cayden's grief in the proper way, but for the life of her, she couldn't figure what else to do. Cayden's therapist said this was all right for short-term coping, but eventually, her son would have to find a healthy way to deal with Tristan being gone.

Though Vivian and Sean had done their best to provide a festive meal—even including Georgia—everyone present missed Tristan to their own degree.

Fortunately, Donna sat at the end of the long table that included Vivian's parents and Tristan's sister, Franny, and her husband and three kids. Brynn couldn't keep from smiling every time she thought of him calling his little sister Fig Newton.

"I don't mind telling you," Donna rambled on, "that every time the phone rings my stomach seizes. Although any truly catastrophic news I'd get through a knock on the door. Anyway, I phoned one of Tristan's friends' wives—Eve. She told me her husband, Garrett, called a month ago and told her everyone on Tristan's team was fine."

As much as Brynn despised the man, she couldn't help but feel shimmery with relief. If she had one Christmas wish above all, as a steady rain tapped the Stoleys' windows, a fire glowed in their hearth and Bing Crosby crooned on their stereo, it was that wherever Tristan and his team happened to be, they were all safe, warm and sharing an equally delicious meal.

"ANOTHER AT TEN!" GARRETT shouted in the black night, firing his weapon blindly behind him. "Move it or lose it, Grinder!"

Tristan ducked to avoid the latest round of gunfire. "Merry freakin' Christmas, huh?"

"Yeah, ho freakin' ho." Arming a grenade, he tossed it deep into the enemy compound they'd raided.

Gunfire rained like New Year's Eve confetti.

Having had enough and spooked by the two of them being cut off from the rest of their team, Tristan let loose with a mighty growl before leaping to his feet and shooting wildly at anything that even remotely moved. "I'm so damned sick of this!"

Round after round he fired into the camp they'd predetermined to be filled with nothing but the lowest of the low of criminals.

With Garrett alongside him, they managed to take out every last one of the men whose résumés included human trafficking, murder, international drug transport and plain old bank robbery.

By the time they met up with their old pal Deacon,

he patted them on their backs. "About time you two showed up for the party."

"Screw you," Tristan said.

Garrett laughed. "Don't mind him. He's just cranky because Santa put nothing in his stocking but drug lords."

"Damn straight." After clearing bodies from the surprisingly plush beehive-style Zulu hut, they all pitched in their favorite condiment packets to add flavor to otherwise disgusting MRE meals.

After dinner, with no water to spare for low-priority tasks like washing, Tristan slept on top of his sleeping bag, dreaming not of a white Christmas, but of being reunited with the people who meant the most.

"TRISTAN…" TWO DAYS AFTER Christmas on a gloomy afternoon, Brynn gripped the phone so tight that the plastic ridges bit her fingers. "Your mom has been worried sick. Why haven't you called?" *I've missed you so bad my heart actually aches.*

"No time to explain. I'm back in Germany, but only for a couple hours. Just needed to touch base. Hear your voice."

Pulse on a runaway course, she closed her eyes, leaning against the kitchen wall for support when her knees threatened to buckle. "Thank you for thinking of me." She hated sounding so formal, but he hadn't left her much choice. What were they? Friends? Lovers, but only when it suited him? His leaving had been breathtakingly cruel. Like a precision mission designed to cause little physical damage, but deliver a crushing psychological blow.

"Not sure if I should say this, but honestly, all I do is think of you—and Mackenzie and Cayden. He around?"

"Yes, but…" She glanced to where her son sat at the kitchen table, icing New Year's Eve cookies for Friday night's big party. The holidays had been especially hard for him—so much so, she'd started taking him to his therapist twice a week. Though she couldn't entirely blame Tristan—Lord knew, Mack's death had played a huge role in messing up their kid—she certainly didn't feel warm and fuzzy where their supposed friend was involved. Cupping the phone's mouthpiece, she whispered, "He's finally getting over you. I'm not sure it'd be wise to open that wound."

"Please…" His ragged tone cut through her every defense. Made her want to hold him, stroking away whatever pained him. "It's been a hellish few days and I could really use a reminder of home."

"Look, Mom!" Cayden held up a yellow-frosted star.

Her stomach knotted.

Cayden had cried for days when Tristan left. He still talked about him all the time. No matter how many times Brynn had gently reminded her son that while Tristan would always be their special friend, he had an important job to do back on his navy base. Sounded good, right? At least until Cayden asked why he wasn't also important to Tristan.

"Brynn…" Tristan's jagged sigh pierced her carefully built walls. "You have to know I never meant for any of this to turn out badly. And I sure didn't want to hurt Cayden."

Since a knot blocked her throat, she nodded. But then felt silly since he couldn't even see her. "Tristan, I—"

"Tristan's on the phone?" Cayden tossed his cookie to the table. Before Brynn could even try stopping him, he'd charged over to grab the handset. "Tristan, hi! I miss you so much! When are you coming home? Even though it's winter, me and Dom practice catching all the time, and when're you coming to see me?"

Though Brynn couldn't hear Tristan's answer, Cayden's slumped shoulders and crestfallen expression told her all she needed to know. Her son was once again in pain, and she was powerless to help. And who did she have to thank for all of this? Tristan.

AFTER TALKING TO TRISTAN, Cayden hung up the phone and tried really hard not to cry.

"Everything all right?" his mom asked.

No! Cayden might've nodded for his mom, but in his hurting belly, he missed Tristan superbad. And he was mad at his mom for letting him go. Why hadn't she stopped him? Had she even asked him to stay in Ruin Bayou to be his dad? Even Mackenzie missed him. Cayden could tell by the way she hardly ever laughed anymore.

"You're awfully quiet over there." At the table, his mom frosted a cookie.

He still stood by the phone.

Mackenzie had been taking a nap, but over her baby monitor she was now screaming.

Cayden said, "I'll get her."

"Thank you, sweetie. That's awfully grown-up of you to help me like that."

"I know." He frowned the whole way up the stairs. What he needed to do was think of a plan to make Tristan come home. Something really big and exciting. He had $23.47 in his piggy bank. Would that be enough to hire one of those skywriter planes like they'd seen on the Fourth of July?

In Mackenzie's room, he scooped her from her crib

and could tell she'd peed in her diaper. He knew how to change that kind, so he did it real fast.

Finished, he sat with her in her big rocking chair. "Wish you weren't just a stupid baby and could talk."

When she smiled at him real big, he felt kinda guilty for calling her stupid.

"If you were bigger—" he jiggled her on his lap "—we could make a plan to get Tristan to come home."

She made one of her cute and funny baby sounds.

"Does that mean you think I should do something by myself?"

Now she made cute noises and kicked.

"I know his navy thing where he works is someplace called Virginia Beach. Think I could ride my bike there in a day?"

Really excited, she wiggled and laughed.

"Maybe it wouldn't even take that long? I'm a really fast rider. All I need to do is make a sandwich and take granola bars and maybe my favorite baseball that Dad gave me that all of his friends signed. Tristan liked it a whole lot, so if I give it to him, then he'll for sure come home."

Cayden jumped when his mom came into the room. "What're you two doing up here?"

"Just talking." He usually asked permission before riding his bike somewhere far—like his friend Dom's house that was two whole blocks away—but this time, he didn't even want his mom to have a chance to say no. All he needed to do was bring back Tristan and his mom and Mac would never do anything but smile again.

Chapter Seventeen

With Cayden spending the night at Dom's and Mackenzie crashing early, Brynn found herself with way more time on her hands than she would've liked. She channel-hopped, but found nothing that held her interest. Turning off the TV, she picked up the novel she'd been wanting to read, but her mind was too busy to focus on even the first page.

Just needed to touch base. Hear your voice.

She should've been encouraged by the fact that Tristan was at least thinking of her and her children, but at best, it came as a hollow victory. So what if he occasionally thought of them? It didn't change the fact that he obviously didn't miss them enough to do anything about it.

She finally fell into a fitful sleep, only to be awakened too early by a violent thunderstorm. Eerie yellow morning light showed high wind had taken a toll on the yard. Leaves and small twigs littered not just the lawn, but her flowerbeds. Looked like Georgia's yard would need a good cleaning, too.

After orange spice tea and a bowl of cereal, she handled all of Mackenzie's morning needs, then packed the baby into her carrier to start work.

By noon, she and Georgia had their yards tidied and

still had time left to help a few other neighbors. Brynn wanted to talk with her friend about Tristan's call, but in the end, she figured what was the point? All the talk in the world wouldn't bring him back. And honestly, did she really even want him back? He'd hurt her so badly. The safest thing for not only her own heart, but her children's would be trying to put Tristan far to the back of their minds.

"Where's Cayden?" Georgia asked, taking off her gardening gloves. "We could've used him this morning."

"He spent the night with Dom. He's usually home by now, though. Maybe Vivian's got him helping out in their yard?"

"Probably." Georgia waved before heading into her home.

Before feeding Mackenzie her lunch, Brynn dialed Vivian's number. "Hey," she said when her friend picked up on the second ring, "just checking in to make sure everything's all right."

After a few minutes of talking about the storm, Brynn said, "What are the boys up to? They've usually ridden their bikes down here by now."

"What do you mean?" Vivian asked. "Dom spent the night with his cousin in Shreveport. We took him yesterday afternoon."

Brynn's pulse raged. "So Cayden hasn't been with you?"

"No…"

Covering her mouth to keep from crying out, Brynn fought to keep calm. There had to be a logical explanation for where Cayden had gone.

Brynn told Vivian she'd call her back, then raced up the stairs to Cayden's room. Maybe once he'd found out Dom was with his cousin, Cayden had come home?

She prayed she'd find him in bed, but all she found was a note on his bed.

Deer Mom, don't wurry I'm bringing Tristan home.

Don't worry?

It was all Brynn could do not to faint.

TRISTAN MADE THE EIGHTEEN-HOUR drive to Shreveport in fourteen. He'd looked into flying, but with scheduling issues, that would've taken even longer.

During the drive, he'd done nothing but pray that by the time he reached Ruin Bayou, Cayden would have already been found—safe.

Worse than the nerves screaming in his stomach was the knowledge that he'd done this. If he'd never left, at this late hour Cayden would be safe in his bed.

He pulled his truck into Brynn's drive at 1:30 a.m. All lights were blazing and cars lined the street—telling him the boy still hadn't been found.

"Tristan…" He hadn't bothered knocking and went inside. His mother ran to him, crushing him in a hug.

Over his mother's head, his gaze met Brynn's. Her eyes were bloodshot and the dark circles beneath told him her terror.

Donna said, "Jason's down at the station, directing searches. I'm sure he'll be grateful for your help."

"I—I have to find Cayden, Mom." Tristan felt as if his whole life had come unhinged. If something unspeakable happened to Brynn's boy, Tristan wasn't sure how he'd live with himself. "If I'd stayed…"

"Stop." His mom gripped his hand. "There'll be enough time for blame once Cayden's found. Until then, do what you've trained for and finish the task at hand."

Brynn had wanted to rail on Tristan as soon as he'd walked through her front door. But how could she be upset with him when she hadn't even called Vivian to check out Cayden's story? All of this could've been avoided with one simple call. Didn't matter that the boys slept over at each other's houses all the time without formal invitation. What mattered was that when Brynn had needed to be a mother most, she'd failed.

She'd set a fresh tray of sandwiches on the dining-room table before seeing Tristan exit not five minutes after his arrival.

Not caring if she looked like a crazy woman, she charged through the subdued crowd, chasing him out the door. "Just like that? You're leaving?"

He was already halfway across the yard, and when he turned to face her, even in faint porch light, she saw he looked no better than her. Red-rimmed eyes and pressed lips told her he cared every bit as much as her about her son. "I'm not leaving, but heading out to bring Cayden home."

Hugging herself, fighting tears, she nodded.

"I'm sorry about all this, Brynn. So sorry."

"Me, too. I know you had to go back to work, but Cayden…" She shrugged. "He didn't understand."

Charging toward her, Tristan wrapped his solid arms around her, and for the first time since realizing Cayden was gone, Brynn felt as if her son really would be okay. He held her and held her, and then kissed her hard before heading for his truck.

Cayden didn't want to cry, but it was getting kind of tough not to. He'd taken a map from his mom's car, but all the lines looked the same.

He'd ridden his bike on the highway for a long time, but once it started thundering, he hid under a bridge. The wind was superscary and all he kept thinking about was how bad he missed his mom and little sister. He missed his dad and Tristan, too, but sometimes he felt guilty that he couldn't remember his dad's face.

By the time the rain ended, it was daytime and so he got back on his bike and kept riding until he saw Virginia's BBQ on a sign in front of a restaurant.

He leaned his bike against the side of the building, then went inside. Only instead of it being like a real place, it was all broken down inside with weeds growing through the floor and lots of broken glass.

Cayden felt really stupid for thinking this was the same Virginia where Tristan lived. He felt even more stupid for not being able to read the map. And this place was smelly—like bunches of wet dogs.

After taking off his backpack, he unzipped it, ate one of the granola bars he'd packed, then sat on the dirty floor, wishing he knew what to do. Should he get back on his bike and ride farther or stand in the road and wait for a policeman to drive by?

A big spider crawled out from under a newspaper.

Cayden scrambled to his feet.

He hated spiders and now, he especially hated this old place. Back on his bike, he rode until his legs ached. But knowing he probably still had a long way to go, he tried not to think about how bad he hurt and instead thought of how awesome it would be once he found Tristan and brought him home. Mackenzie would be so excited, but especially his mom. She and Tristan could get married and they'd be a family again, back like it used to be before his dad died.

TEN FRUITLESS HOURS INTO HIS search, Tristan tried thinking like a little kid. What would Jack have done in a situation like this?

Tristan returned to Brynn's house, only not to go inside, but to hopefully get his mind wrapped around the route Cayden may have taken. Tristan left the neighborhood, aiming for the nearest highway—or what Cayden may have perceived as a big road. Once there, he fought to squelch crushing waves of hopelessness and fear. Those kinds of things weren't in his nature, so why, when he most needed a cool head, was he losing it?

Think, Tristan. Think.

Going on pure gut feel, he turned east, and kept heading east until reaching the small town of Perry. Once there, he asked around in a few shops and a gas station if they'd seen a kid, showing them Cayden's most recent school photo. All said no, until a gas station attendant said he'd seen a boy riding by himself on his way into work that morning and thought it odd he was out that far on his own.

Tristan thanked the man, then climbed back in his truck, searching, searching for what he didn't know.

Twenty minutes later, he eyed an old abandoned barbecue joint with the name Virginia on the burned-out sign. Following a hunch that Cayden may have thought there was a connection between this Virginia and the one where Tristan lived, he parked his truck and went inside.

The place reeked of mildew and piss.

His footsteps crunching on broken glass, Tristan did a room-by-room search only to come up empty.

He'd circled back to the main room, taking one last look before leaving when a glimmer on the floor caught his gaze. He knelt to pick up the wrapper from one of the Scooby-Doo granola bars Cayden favored.

Tristan held it to his nose to find the grainy scent still fresh. Heart racing, he bolted for the door.

A few minutes later, he found bike tracks. Once he located the spot where Cayden had left the dirt lot to get back on the asphalt, Tristan hopped back in the truck, searching the shoulder as he traveled farther down the desolate road.

Ten minutes after that, he spotted Cayden, perched on a metal guardrail, knees scraped and crying, but otherwise in good shape.

Tristan veered the truck onto the shoulder, slamming it into Park, then jumped out to lift the boy into his arms. "Don't *ever* run away again," he managed to choke out past his throat that had tightened with tears. Holding Cayden close, Tristan drank in his familiar, little boy smell. "You scared your mother and me something fierce."

"I—I'm sorry," Cayden sobbed through sloppy tears. "I was scared, too. L-last night there was a really bad storm and I knew alligators were gonna eat me. I missed Mom and you and even M-Mac…" The boy clung to Tristan, making his chest ache with emotion. How could he have ever left this beautiful child? Yet in the same respect, how could he risk his heart on Brynn one day taking him away just as Andrea had done with Jack? Tristan honestly feared he wouldn't survive that kind of pain.

"Mom!"

Brynn's knees buckled with relief upon seeing her son leap from Tristan's truck cab. Gripping the porch rail for support, she forced deep breaths, welcoming the relief of happy tears. In a heartbeat, he'd run into her arms and she clung to him, kissing the top of his sweet, sweet head.

"I'm sorry, Mom. I promise I'll never run away again."

There'd been so much she'd planned to say, delivering a lecture he wouldn't soon forget. But now, all she could focus on was how grateful she was to Tristan for bringing him home.

When the crush of neighbors jockeying to see Cayden and hear his adventure had finally lessened, Brynn felt secure enough to leave him on his own for a short while to properly acknowledge what Tristan had done.

"How can I ever repay you?" she asked past a fresh batch of tears.

"No need. Anyone could've found him. I got lucky that it was me." Was she imagining things, or did he seem reluctant to meet her gaze?

"Tristan, if you think this changes anything—that I expect you to stay, you can relax. I understand you can't make a commitment to us and I refuse to settle for less."

Jaw clenched, he nodded. "What about Cayden?"

"He's been in counseling. Trust me, after this stunt, he'll no doubt have plenty more. But eventually, I have to believe he'll be okay."

"I'm sorry."

"That you can't trust me? That you can't give more?"

"Stop…" His tone was uncharacteristically low.

"Why? You're the one apologizing. That means something. That you feel something." More than anything, she wanted to cling to him, fisting his shirt while kissing him breathless. But what was the point? He was still scared and after what Mack had put her through by not communicating, the last thing she needed in her life was another man who was too thickheaded to talk.

"BUT I THOUGHT NOW THAT YOU were here," Cayden asked Tristan at the breakfast table the next morning, "that you were going to stay?"

"Wish I could," Tristan said, "but my CO called and said he needs me back on base."

"What's that?" Cayden wrinkled his nose.

"It means he's my commanding officer—or boss. If I don't do what he says, I'll go to jail."

"Oh." While pushing his pancakes around in the syrup, Cayden felt sadder than he had in a real long time. When Tristan rescued him, he thought that meant he wanted to be his new dad.

"Next time there's a holiday, I'll be back. Maybe I can bring my son. You'd like him." Cayden flinched when Tristan ruffled his hair. He wasn't a baby and he hated it when grown-ups treated him like one.

"If you don't like us anymore," Cayden said, "you don't have to lie. Just go away and stop making my mom and me cry."

"Cayden…"

His mom came and stood behind him. "Tristan, I think it'd be best if you go."

"Yeah." Cayden held his mom's hand real tight. He loved Tristan and more than anything wanted him to be his dad, but running taught him Virginia Beach was too far away to get to on his bike. Even worse, no matter what Cayden said or did, it wasn't going to be enough to make Tristan come home.

"DOING ANYTHING SPECIAL FOR Valentine's Day?" Brynn's boss, Lindsay, asked while they finished planting the last of the potted Christmas trees that hadn't sold over the holidays. It'd been so rainy for the past few weeks, the ground had been too muddy to dig.

"Ha! You're so funny." Brynn bore down extra hard on her shovel. When Tristan left after helping find Cayden she'd hoped it would be easier saying goodbye a second time, but if anything, it'd been harder.

"I'm not trying to be. But, sugar, the man dumped you going on nearly six months ago. You can't just sit around pining for him forever."

"Who said I'm pining? I'm up early every morning, getting my kid to school on time and myself to work. My baby's clean and fed—"

"Not to mention, cute as a bug in a rug in that new sweater." She grinned at Mackenzie, who sat in her stroller, gnawing a rattle.

"You're missing my point. If I were truly pining for Tristan, wouldn't I do nothing but sit around in my pj's all day? Eating bonbons and listening to Barry Manilow?"

"I don't know." Lindsay grunted while lifting an extra-full shovel of dirt. "I've always been a fan of Celine Dion when I'm blue, but that's beside the point. I ran into Vivian at the bank the other day, and she told me a while back Sean's firm hired a lawyer who's single, and—"

"Stop right there." Brynn rested against her shovel. "My so-called friend has been trying to hook me up with this guy practically since the day Tristan left. When— if—I'm interested, I'll be sure to let you both know."

Lindsay rolled her eyes. "Now you're missing my point. This guy's hot, can afford to buy you a nice steak at Scooter's and still has his own teeth. Sounds like a winning combination to me."

"Nah…" Grinning, Brynn shook her head. "I only go for the geriatric set who've lost all their teeth."

Lindsay stuck out her tongue, then allowed Brynn to

finish the task in welcome silence save for the wind in the pines and Mackenzie's happy babble.

It'd been so long since Tristan had been gone, when she closed her eyes she had a tough time remembering his face. But when she dreamed?

Raw emotion threatened to overwhelm her.

Oh, when she dreamed, the man played a starring role in brilliant Technicolor. But what did that matter? Even if by some miracle he showed up on her doorstep, begging for her to take him back, would she? Considering how Cayden had fared during his absence, no. And like Tristan's mom, Brynn had been a nervous wreck, consumed by fears of what she'd do were she to hear that one of his missions had gone horribly wrong.

"TRISTAN, GOOD TO SEE YOU." His CO, Mark Hewitt, welcomed him into his office. The room's only decor was a cheap plastic ivy the team had bought him one year for his birthday since his every attempt at growing a real plant always ended in disaster. Sleet sounded like tacks hitting the window. "You did a helluva job our last trip out."

"Thank you, Chief." Tristan had been back in the country for a week, but had yet to even call his mom. He'd been working on a plan with Deacon, Garret and Calder, but wanted to officially explore his options first.

"So, to what do I owe this visit?"

"Permission to speak freely, sir?" He wiped sweating palms on the thighs of his camos.

"Granted."

"First, let me just say I love the navy. From the day I enlisted, there was never anything else I wanted to do."

Commander Hewitt nodded. "That's why I'm glad to have you on my team."

"That's just it, sir. In Somalia at Christmas, something in me snapped and I—" he bowed his head "—I'm not proud of myself, but I lost it. In this case, my anger worked in our favor, and I got lucky in that no civilians were around, but I was just so pissed." He leaned forward, looking the man he greatly respected in his eyes. "I hated these freakin' assholes who cause all of us to be away from our families for so much time and for what? It's like we take out one bad guy and four more grow in his place."

"True." A nerve ticked in the commander's jaw. "But that's what we signed up to do. And if we weren't out there in the world's shit holes, taking care of business, can you even imagine how much worse off the planet would be?"

"I get that. No one understands the importance of SEALs more than me. Which is why I need to run something by you...."

Chapter Eighteen

The Tuesday before his big Valentine's Day party, Cayden was in music class when a student aide handed him a pink slip that made him have to go to the office. He didn't think he'd done anything wrong, but all his friends made the *oooooo* sound anyway.

All the way there, his stomach felt like he might need to barf.

Outside the office, the principal, Mrs. Dega, stood waiting for him. She wore her meanest look and his heart beat so hard he almost ran back to class. "Hello, Cayden."

"Um, hi?"

She put her hand on his back, guiding him to the bulletin board his mom sometimes helped decorate for PTA. "Sorry to take you from music, but there's someone here to see you. He's not family, but I know from several sources he's an extremely close family friend. I would ordinarily call your mother to obtain her permission for him to speak with you, but in this case, my instincts tell me it'll be okay."

Nose wrinkled, Cayden asked, "What's 'obb-taned' mean? And who wants to see me so bad he's brave enough to sit alone in your scary office?"

She actually laughed! "We'll worry about word definitions later. Right now, I just need to know if you'd like to see your old friend Tristan?"

"He's here?"

Nodding, she said, "Yes, sir. He's come a long way just to see you."

Cayden nibbled at the inside of his bottom lip. Part of him wanted to see Tristan more than anything in the whole world. Another part was still mad at him for leaving.

"Cayden? If you'd rather not visit with him, you're free to return to class."

"I will…"

"See Tristan or go to class?"

He took the deepest, bravest breath he knew how. "I guess I probably want to see Tristan."

"Hey, bud." Tristan stood when Cayden entered the room. The principal thankfully gave them some privacy by shutting her door. The blinds on her window-wall remained open. "I missed you."

The boy just stood there, staring.

"Sorry I haven't called. I've been in Africa twice this year."

Cayden took a moment to ponder this, then asked, "Did you see an anaconda?"

"No, but I did see a lioness with her cubs."

"That's cool."

"Know what else I saw every day while I was gone?"

Shaking his head, Cayden said, "Nope."

From the chest pocket of his khaki shirt, Tristan withdrew two worn photos. One of Jack and the other of Cayden, Mackenzie and their mom. Handing them both to the boy, Tristan said, "On every mission I've taken since being away from you—especially since you ran away—I looked at these every morning when I got up and every night before going to sleep. I missed you guys a lot."

Notching his chin higher, Cayden said in a surprisingly grown-up tone, "I missed you. So did Mom. She cried lots when she thought I wasn't looking, but I was."

"I'm sorry," was all Tristan could think to say. Deeply, profoundly sorry.

"Okay."

"I never meant to hurt you, but I was confused. I know that's not a good enough reason for what I did, but that's all I've got. Guess what I need to know is can you forgive me? And if you can—" he fished in his jeans pocket withdrawing a small box "—would you be okay with me giving this to your mom, then asking her to be my Valentine?"

"Whoa!" Cayden said when Tristan opened Brynn's gift. "That's *really* pretty."

"I thought so. But do you think she'll like it enough to marry me so I can be your stepdad?"

Tears welled in both of their eyes when Cayden nodded, then crushed Tristan in a hug. "Please don't leave me again."

More than anything, Tristan wished he could deliver that promise now, but before that, he had one more stop.

"Aw, sweetie, please eat," Brynn all but begged Mackenzie the morning of Valentine's Day. "We've got to get cookies and cupcakes to your brother's party by eleven and judging by how much oatmeal you've put in your pretty curls, it's going to take that long just to wash your hair."

"Baaaa!" Mackenzie said in answer to her mother's request. *"Baaaa! Baaaa!"* Grinning, she proudly dis-

played her three teeth while kicking the footrest of her high chair.

"Okey doke." Brynn removed the plastic tray and hefted her big girl from her seat. "I'm taking that as a sign you're through."

She was on her way to the tub with her sticky daughter when the doorbell rang.

"Who in the world is that?" she asked Mackenzie. "We don't have time for a magazine salesman."

Beyond the front door window was a bright, sunny day, and Brynn couldn't make out much more than the silhouette of a man. She pulled back the curtain only to gasp.

Tristan?

Pulse racing to an alarming degree, she wasn't sure whether to laugh, cry or bolt.

"Brynn," he called through the door. "Please, let me in."

She ran her hands through her hair and then groaned at her misbuttoned nightgown. In all the times she'd imagined this very scene, she'd never been quite so disheveled.

She unlatched the dead bolt. Door open, she hadn't a clue what to say.

"Baaaah!" Mackenzie was all too happy to do the talking.

"Wow, has she grown." Tristan gazed at the baby in awe. "I've missed out on so much."

Yes, you have, it was on the tip of Brynn's tongue to snap, but what was the point? Judging by the tears in his eyes, Tristan knew exactly what he'd missed out on by running.

"Mind if I hold her?"

"She's covered in oatmeal. I was just going upstairs to give her a bath."

He took the baby anyway, cradling her close, pressing a tender kiss to her forehead.

Part of Brynn envied Mackenzie's kiss, but another part wished Tristan would just blurt out whatever was on his mind, then leave. He'd already caused her more than enough sleepless nights.

"I've been dreaming of this day ever since the last time I walked out the door."

"Oh?" She perched on the sofa arm.

"I thought I'd make a big Valentine declaration. Buy you dozens of roses and more chocolate than you could eat in a year, but the way we left things, somehow I figured simple and straight-to-the-point was best."

He'd hurt her so badly, she refused to even look at him. "I don't mean to be rude," she said, "but I don't have anything to say to you. After you found Cayden, I told you what I wanted, and if you can't provide at least some level of commitment to me then—"

"Woman, anyone ever tell you, you talk a lot?" From the pocket of his jeans, he withdrew a burgundy velvet box that'd been tied with a crushed white satin bow. He handed it to her. "Before you say anything else, open this. Sorry about the ribbon. Guess I should've planned better for that contingency."

She opened the box only to have her vision blur by tears for him that she'd sworn she'd given up. The square-cut diamond was everything she'd ever dreamed of in an engagement ring, just as Tristan had the potential to be her perfect groom. But potential was all he'd ever be because he knew she couldn't marry him while he held such a dangerous job.

"I see your mind working and before you say a word

about your fear of me being gunned down, hear me out. I'm still a SEAL, but assuming you're okay with California, I've already filed for a transfer to be an instructor at the SEAL training center in Coronado. Not only will I be home every night for dinner, but we can spend weekends with Jack. Hell, we can even bring my mom out to live with us if you want—but only if you want."

More tears started and wouldn't stop.

But then laughter won when Mackenzie took charge of the situation, poking Tristan's right ear. *"Baaaahhh!"*

"Ouch," he said to her daughter. "You're kind of ruining my big proposal here."

"I don't know," Brynn said, "I kind of like the look of oatmeal in your hair." Clenching his ring in one hand, she cupped his handsome face with her other. Was this truly happening? After all her lonely months of hoping and praying he'd not only return, but return with a way for them to both be happy, he'd done just that, making her wildest dreams come true. But it wasn't just her making this decision. Cayden also needed a say.

"At least you still think I look good, but I'm waiting for an answer, Brynn. I'm so sorry for leaving the way I did. But now I know beyond any shadow of doubt that us being an official family is right."

"But is it?" Pacing, she said, "What about Cayden? You didn't just hurt me. How's he going to feel about being uprooted again?"

"Fine."

"What do you mean?" Her eyes narrowed. "Without personally asking him, how would you know?"

"Because I did—ask him." He removed Mackenzie's sticky fingers from his ear once more. "In fact, I spent a good portion of yesterday afternoon not only asking his forgiveness, but for your hand in marriage and permission to cart all of you out to the west coast."

"And he was okay with it?" She was almost afraid to ask.

"Would I lie?"

No. Tristan might infuriate or delight, but deception wasn't his style. If anything, at times he'd been too brutally honest.

He set Mackenzie in the nearby playpen. Taking her hand, he uncurled her fingers from around his ring box. He opened it, removed the bauble, then held it between his thumb and forefinger. On bended knee, mesmerizing her with just his white-toothed smile, he said, "I love you. I love you more than I ever thought it possible to love. I love your son and your sticky daughter. I even love the way you're so cautious with your heart and your children's that you're making me wait forever to answer my very simple question."

"I can't," she squeaked through a fresh batch of tears.

"Baby..." He was back on his feet, kissing her cheeks and nose and finally, finally her lips. "Why not?"

"I know it sounds silly, but I'm afraid this is too good to be real. I'm afraid you're standing here, kissing me breathless, is nothing but a lovely dream. I can't wake up alone again, Tristan. I can't breathe without you."

He slipped the ring on her finger. "Which is why we might want to get married sooner as opposed to later."

"Stop." Hands pressed to his strong chest, she said, "Don't make light of this moment."

"I'm not." He kissed her again, only to be interrupted by a cooing, gurgling monkey crawling between them.

"Baaa! Baaa! Baaahhh!"

He looked down. "Did she just..."

"Escape her playpen without assistance? Afraid so.

Your parenting duties are suddenly about to be way more difficult than when you left."

"Not a problem." He swooped the baby into his arms. "I may no longer be on the front line of SEAL action, but I'll never back down from a challenge. Especially female challenges with crazy-beautiful blue eyes, freckles and oatmeal in their curly red hair."

Epilogue

From the patio of the Malibu beach house a friend loaned them for the weekend, Tristan watched Jack and Cayden build a sand fort on the beach.

Cayden had been seeing a new therapist for a while, and seemed to grow stronger every day in not only adjusting to what happened to his dad, but understanding that life was always changing—and sometimes, that change was actually pretty darn good.

In the kitchen, Donna and a very pregnant Brynn verbally brawled over whether to use applesauce in the breakfast muffins or butter. For once, it was his über-healthy mom battling on the side of good food versus evil—not that butter was bad, per se, but he wanted her with them for as long as possible.

This weekend was a celebration of Brynn and his one-year wedding anniversary. Their ceremony had been simple, but heartfelt, held in Donna's lush garden in front of family and friends. Fig Newton had even come down for the occasion.

Newly tech-savvy Georgia, who'd gone in on a San Diego condo with his mom, joined him on the patio, slapping an email she'd just printed on the porch rail. "Would you look at this? I just got it from our agent. Your mother and I have four casting calls next week—

four. How are we supposed to volunteer at the botanical gardens *and* keep up with our careers?" With a sharp exhale, she sat in the seat beside him. "Is the man nuts? I know we're talented and all, but there's only so much of us to go around."

Tristan tried taking her concerns seriously, but ended up laughing, which only earned him a swat with the email.

Brynn finally emerged from the kitchen to wrap her arms around him from behind. In his ear she whispered, "Your mom found a neighbor to chat up. If we hurry, we can get the boys to watch Mac while we...*you know.*"

"I heard that," Georgia said. "You two go on. Not that my plate isn't already full enough, I'll just add babysitting to my already hectic schedule."

"Love you." Brynn kissed the white-haired woman's wrinkled cheek.

"Love you, too," she said to Tristan's wife. "You, however," she said to him, "are fresh—not to mention, inconsiderate to your elders. And there's still that matter to clear up about the bubble gum you stole from my store. If you weren't so darned good-looking, I'd have erased you from my Facebook friend list a long while back."

Brynn gasped, then laughed. "Georgia! Are you crushing on my husband?"

"No way. Bob Barker's more my type."

Tristan tried keeping a straight face, but failed. "If I have to lose you," he teased, "at least it's to a worthy opponent."

She cast him the same dirty look she used to when he and Mack caused trouble in his yard. "Brynn, you'd better get him out of my sight before I change my mind about watching the kids."

"Come on…" Brynn held out her hand to help Tristan from his chair, only she looked so cute with flour on her left cheek and her hair in a crooked pigtail, he ended up pulling her onto his lap for a kiss right then and there.

"Eeeeuw!" the boys shouted from the beach.

Mackenzie, seated on the far side of the porch surrounded by naked Barbies, didn't even look up.

"I concur," Georgia noted from her chair.

"I don't know…" Brynn kissed him again. "Mr. Bartoni, I kind of like your kisses."

"'Kind of'?"

"Maybe I could better judge under more private conditions?"

"Woman—" he pushed her upright from his lap, then took her hand, leading her to the stairs "—at this point, your approval is no longer an issue. Like it or not, you're stuck with me for a good, long while."

Midway up the stairs, she wrapped her arms around his neck, stealing one more kiss. "Mmm…I wouldn't have it any other way."

* * * * *

Be sure to look for more stories in
Laura Marie Altom's
OPERATION: FAMILY *series in 2013!*

REQUEST YOUR FREE BOOKS!
2 FREE NOVELS PLUS 2 FREE GIFTS!

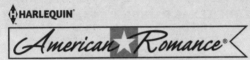

HARLEQUIN

American ★ Romance

LOVE, HOME & HAPPINESS

YES! Please send me 2 FREE Harlequin® American Romance® novels and my 2 FREE gifts (gifts are worth about $10). After receiving them, if I don't wish to receive any more books, I can return the shipping statement marked "cancel." If I don't cancel, I will receive 4 brand-new novels every month and be billed just $4.49 per book in the U.S. or $5.24 per book in Canada. That's a savings of at least 14% off the cover price! It's quite a bargain! Shipping and handling is just 50¢ per book in the U.S. and 75¢ per book in Canada.* I understand that accepting the 2 free books and gifts places me under no obligation to buy anything. I can always return a shipment and cancel at any time. Even if I never buy another book, the two free books and gifts are mine to keep forever.

154/354 HDN FVPK

Name	(PLEASE PRINT)	
Address		Apt. #
City	State/Prov.	Zip/Postal Code

Signature (if under 18, a parent or guardian must sign)

Mail to the **Harlequin® Reader Service:**
IN U.S.A.: P.O. Box 1867, Buffalo, NY 14240-1867
IN CANADA: P.O. Box 609, Fort Erie, Ontario L2A 5X3

Want to try two free books from another line?
Call 1-800-873-8635 or visit www.ReaderService.com.

* Terms and prices subject to change without notice. Prices do not include applicable taxes. Sales tax applicable in N.Y. Canadian residents will be charged applicable taxes. Offer not valid in Quebec. This offer is limited to one order per household. Not valid for current subscribers to Harlequin American Romance books. All orders subject to credit approval. Credit or debit balances in a customer's account(s) may be offset by any other outstanding balance owed by or to the customer. Please allow 4 to 6 weeks for delivery. Offer available while quantities last.

Your Privacy—The Harlequin® Reader Service is committed to protecting your privacy. Our Privacy Policy is available online at www.ReaderService.com or upon request from the Harlequin Reader Service.

We make a portion of our mailing list available to reputable third parties that offer products we believe may interest you. If you prefer that we not exchange your name with third parties, or if you wish to clarify or modify your communication preferences, please visit us at www.ReaderService.com/consumerschoice or write to us at Harlequin Reader Service Preference Service, P.O. Box 9062, Buffalo, NY 14269. Include your complete name and address.

HARI3

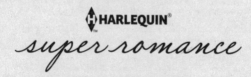